FROM HATE TO LOVE

Never had Atayla seen a man looking so angry, and before she could speak, before she could think or ask what he was doing, the Earl said:

"I am well aware of why you came here, Miss Lindsay, and why my wife sent you to seduce me into giving her the divorce she needs."

"What are you . . . saying? How . . . dare you. . . ."

"You can go back to my wife and tell her that you have been unable to carry out your instructions."

"Please," she pleaded, "please . . . let me . . . explain."

"I have no intention of listening to your lies!" He almost spat the words at her. Then he was aware that she was trembling, that her eyes were looking up at him, her hair shimmering in the light of the candles.

His arms went round her, he pulled her against him and his lips came down on hers. He kissed her roughly, and she was completely helpless in his arms. . . .

Bantam Books by Barbara Cartland
Ask your bookseller for the books you have missed

Barbara Cartland's Library of Love Series

From Hate to Love

Barbara Cartland

BANTAM BOOKS
TORONTO · NEW YORK · LONDON · SYDNEY

FROM HATE TO LOVE
A Bantam Book / December 1982

ISBN 0-553-23161-8

Published simultaneously in the United States and Canada

Bantam Books are published by Bantam Books, Inc. Its trademark,
consisting of the words "Bantam Books" and the portrayal of a rooster,
is Registered in U.S. Patent and Trademark Office and in other
countries. Marca Registrada. Bantam Books, Inc., 666 Fifth Avenue,
New York, New York 10103.

PRINTED IN THE UNITED STATES OF AMERICA

O   0 9 8 7 6 5 4 3 2 1

Author's Note

The indissolubility of marriage was part of the doctrine of the Christian Church from early times, and it was held that all sexual activity outside marriage was suspect.

The first breach in this doctrine was made by the Protestant Reformers who regarded it as permissible for a man to repudiate an adulterous wife and, even if she was not put to death by the executioner, to marry again.

Sometime later, adultery by the husband if coupled with severe cruelty was recognised as grounds for a wife to seek the termination of a marriage.

In contrast to the non-Roman Catholic Churches in Scotland and on the Continent of Europe, the Church of England was less progressive and still upheld the doctrine of indissolubility. Eventually Parliament assumed the power to dissolve marriage. However, this was so expensive a procedure that the total number of divorces granted by Parliament between 1602 and 1859 was only 317.

In 1837, after heated debates it became lawful for a husband to obtain a judicial divorce from a wife guilty of adultery. But a wife had to prove that her husband's adultery was aggravated by cruelty or vice. This provision was not rescinded until 1923.

The power of the King's Proctor to intervene during the six-month period between the *decree nisi* and the *decree absolute* was very unpopular, but continued until the Divorce Reform Act of 1969.

From Hate to Love

Chapter One
1899

"You're late! If you want something to eat, you'd better get it yourself! I'm not here to wait on you. I've got other things to do!"

As she spoke, the elderly woman, who was half-Spanish, half-Arab, walked out of the kitchen and slammed the door.

Atayla sighed, having expected this reaction.

Her first impulse was to go without food, but then her common sense told her that this would be a very stupid thing to do.

After she had been so ill with the wound in her shoulder, she knew that what she needed now was what any Doctor would call "building up" in order to regain her strength.

But this was difficult in a religious household where every other day seemed to be a Fast Day, and Mrs. Mansur, Housekeeper to Father Ignatius, was extremely hostile.

When Atayla had first been brought to the Mission in Tangiers, she was unconscious, and it was some time before she realised where she was or could remember what had happened.

Then the whole horror of the sudden attack by the desert robbers upon herself and her father as they were

1

making their way towards Tangiers seemed like a nightmare from which she could not awaken.

It seemed extraordinary, after Gordon Lindsay had travelled all over North Africa without coming to any harm, although there had been moments of danger, that when he was almost within sight of Tangiers at the end of his latest expedition, disaster had struck.

It might have been anticipated, Atayla thought now, as she remembered how few servants they had with them, because in the first place one of their camels had died and the other had been too weak to make the journey home, and secondly they could not afford to buy replacements.

The result was that she was now destitute.

Her father was dead and she was penniless, but she had to pull herself together and work out how she could get back to England, and once there find some of her father's relatives and hope they would look after her until she could find employment of some sort.

It was all too much of an effort!

She felt so weak and her head seemed to be stuffed full of cotton-wool, so that she felt unable to use her brain and think things out sensibly and clearly.

She looked round the airless, low-ceilinged kitchen and wondered what she should eat.

Last week, when she had first been able to get out of bed, she was aware that the Housekeeper not only grudged her every mouthful she ate, but was also wildly jealous because Father Ignatius, for whom she had an admiration that was almost idolatrous, talked to her.

An elderly man, kind and extremely sympathetic to all those who came to him in trouble, Father Ignatius ran the Mission.

It consisted of Catholic Missionaries who had training in medicine, and they went out to preach the Gospel to the Arab tribes, who in most cases had no wish to listen to them.

But the Missionaries' lives were dedicated to converting the heathen, and if they suffered intolerable hardships and sometimes premature death in the process, they would undoubtedly be accepted in Heaven with open arms.

But such ideals apparently had not communicated themselves to the Housekeeper. Atayla knew that she must make plans to leave, and decided she would talk about it to Father Ignatius that evening after supper.

Because she would be eating with him, she would at least have something of a square meal, unless, of course, it was a Fast Day.

In the meantime, she was hungry, and she remembered that last night had been one of the evenings on which a long grace was said over two slices of coarse bread, and there had been nothing else for supper except a glass of water.

She opened the cupboards in the kitchen and found a very small egg, which, because it was pushed to the back behind some cups, she was sure Mrs. Mansur had deliberately hidden from her.

She put it on the kitchen-table, then found a loaf of stale bread, from which she cut herself a thick slice and toasted it in front of the range, in which the fire had almost died out.

It all took time, and by the time she had poached the egg and put it on the bread she was no longer hungry.

But because she had had much experience in coping with illness during her travels with her father, she forced herself to eat, and when the last crumb was finished she knew that she felt a little stronger.

"What I should really enjoy," she told herself, "is a fat chicken that has been roasted in the oven, some fresh vegetables from an English garden, and new potatoes."

Then she laughed at the idea. It seemed so out of keeping with the brilliant sunshine outside, which was really too hot at midday to be enjoyable.

She sat at the table with the empty plate in front of

her and told herself that now was the moment when she must plan her future.

There was just a chance that her father's publishers, if she could get in touch with them, would give her a small advance on the latest manuscript which her father had sent them only a month ago.

By the mercy of God, it had not been with them when the robbers had left them for dead and made off with everything they possessed.

They had even stripped her father of his clothing, Atayla subsequently learnt, but they did not touch her, apart from stabbing her in the shoulder, and had left her unconscious.

The horses they had been riding and the one camel they had left, which was worth at least a hundred pounds and had been carrying all their worldly possessions, had vanished.

Atayla was left with just what she "stood up in" and, as she said herself, not even a penny to bless herself with.

She started worrying that even if the publishers did give her a small advance, it would not be enough for her fare to England, and she would have to throw herself on the mercy of the British Consul.

But when she had suggested this to Father Ignatius, he had not been very optimistic.

From what he said, she gathered that there were far too many English people who found themselves stranded in North Africa because they had either been robbed or had lost their money through sheer carelessness, and the British Consul helped them back to their own country only under very extenuating circumstances.

Atayla considered that her father, having a fine reputation amongst scholars, might come into this category.

At the same time, every instinct in her body shied away from asking for charity and doubtless having to submit to an humiliating cross-examination as to why her father was not better off.

While scholars like himself, and explorers who acknowledged him to be an authority, would understand, it would be quite a different thing to explain to some Senior Clerk that her father had dedicated his life to research into the tribes of North Africa, especially the Berbers.

As very little was known about these people, and since so much about their history, their religion, and their habits was secret, Gordon Lindsay knew that he was contributing something of great importance to historical research.

'Perhaps when Papa's book is published,' Atayla thought, 'he will be acclaimed as he should have been in his lifetime.'

At the same time, she had the dismal idea that as in the case of other books he had written and articles he had contributed to the Royal Geographical Society and the *Société des Géographes*, only a chosen few would appreciate his discoveries, and his sales would be infinitesimal.

'I will have to rely on myself,' Atayla thought, and wondered what qualifications she had for earning money.

That she could speak Arabic and a number of African dialects was hardly a saleable ability if she returned to England.

At the same time, she knew it would be impossible for her to live alone in any part of Africa, and she had the uncomfortable feeling that if she stayed in the Mission, or in any other place that catered for unattached young women, she would come up against the same hostility that she was experiencing in the house of Father Ignatius.

Her mother, before she died, had said to her:

"You are going to be very lovely, my darling, just as Papa and I always thought you would be. But you will have to face the truth that a beautiful woman always pays a penalty for her looks."

Atayla had not understood, and her mother had smiled as she went on:

"There will be men who will pursue you, and women who will hate you. I can only hope, my dearest, that you will find a man who will make you as happy as I have been with your father."

"Have you really been happy, Mama," Atayla had asked, "without a proper home, always wandering, always moving from one place to another?"

Just for a moment there had been a radiant expression on her mother's face before she answered:

"I think it would be impossible for any woman to be as happy as I have been! Everything I have done with your father has been so exciting, and even when things have been desperate, uncomfortable, and dangerous, we have always managed to laugh."

That was true, Atayla thought, for when her mother had died it seemed as if the laughter had gone out of her father's life and hers.

She had tried desperately to take her mother's place in looking after him and seeing that he had proper meals, and making their journeys from place to place, sometimes across unknown, uncharted deserts, a happy adventure.

But while her father had loved her and she loved him, she had always known that he missed her mother desperately.

Although he still laughed, the spontaneity and the joy had been left behind in an unmarked grave in an Arab village that was so small it did not even have a name.

Once or twice during their married life her father and mother had returned to England, and she had been born there.

They had gone back six years ago, when her mother's father had died, and Atayla had met a number of relations, all of whom disapproved of her father and the life he led.

Because she had been only twelve at the time, it

was hard to remember them at all clearly, but she was sure that they would not welcome her with any enthusiasm if she arrived orphaned and penniless on their doorstep.

Her father's relatives lived in the far North of England on the border of Scotland.

It was perhaps his Scottish blood which had made him an adventurer, and his North Country brain which had made him a writer.

Atayla remembered now that, although his parents were dead, he had a brother who was older than he was and from whom he had not heard for several years.

She had the uncomfortable feeling that he might be dead. There was also a sister who was married, but try as she would she could not remember her married name.

The only thing to do, she told herself practically, would be to go North and look for them.

Then she asked herself how she could find the money to do that.

It was depressing now to remember that her father, before they had set off on their last expedition, had drawn everything he possessed, which was only a few hundred pounds, out of the Bank in Tangiers.

He had spent most of it on the animals and servants they required for their journey, but when they were on the way back he reckoned that there was enough money left to keep them in comfort for a month or so when they reached Tangiers.

"What we will do," he said, "is rent ourselves a small house on the outskirts of the town, and the two articles I intend to write for the *Société des Géographes,* who are always interested in Africa, will bring in quite a good sum. Then we must decide, my dearest, what to do next."

Atayla had not worried. She was used to what her mother called "living from hand to mouth" and was content to accept her father's optimism that something would "turn up," as it invariably had.

But now her father was not there, and for the first

time in her life she was really frightened about the future.

She had sat so long in thought at the kitchen-table that she started when she heard the front door open and knew it was Father Ignatius returning.

Quickly she jumped to her feet and put her plate in the sink, meaning to wash it up later, and went from the kitchen to speak to him.

A good-looking man of nearly sixty, with deep lines on his face and eyes tired from overwork, Atayla knew he found the sun too strong in the middle of the day, which was why he had returned to the Mission to rest in the small room he had fitted up as a Study.

As Atayla appeared, he smiled, put down his flat clerical hat with its wide brim, and said:

"Ah, there you are, my child. I want to talk to you."

"And I want to talk to you, Father, if you have the time."

"Then let us go into my Study," Father Ignatius suggested. "It will be cooler there."

"Can I get you something to drink?" Atayla asked.

"A glass of water would be very refreshing."

Atayla went into the kitchen and, having poured some water into a glass, found one withered lime in the wicker basket which should have contained fruit.

She sliced it and squeezed what little juice there was into the water, hoping it would at least give it a pleasant taste.

She knew it was what her father would have wanted, but she had the feeling that Father Ignatius, deep in his thoughts and prayers, would hardly have noticed if she had poured him a glass of champagne.

She took the water to where he was already seated in one of the worn bamboo chairs that had seen better days, and he took the glass from her absentmindedly and drank a little as she sat down beside him.

"You are too tired to talk now," Atayla said. "I will let you rest and come back in an hour."

"I think the person who should be resting is you," Father Ignatius replied. "How do you feel?"

"Better," Atayla answered, "and the wound on my shoulder has healed, although it does not look very pretty. But as no-one is likely to see it, it is of no particular importance."

She spoke lightly, hoping that Father Ignatius would smile, but he was staring ahead of him. Then, as if he had not even heard what she said, he said:

"I have a proposition to put to you, Atayla, although I am not certain it is the right thing for me to do."

Atayla was surprised by his tone of voice, and she answered:

"If it is a proposition by which I can make some money, Father, you know it is something I have to consider. Everything Papa possessed was taken by the robbers, and I can only be grateful that the manuscript of his last book was already on its way to England."

"We should certainly thank God that it is safe," Father Ignatius replied, "and that you, my child, did not lose your life, which is a more precious possession than anything else."

"I agree, Father," Atayla answered. "At the same time, as you are well aware, I now have to keep myself, or at least make enough money so that I can return to England and find Papa's relatives, if they are still alive."

There was a little silence. Then Father Ignatius said:

"That is what I want to tell you about. God indeed often moves in mysterious ways."

Atayla waited, her eyes on his face, knowing he did not like to be hurried when he had something to relate.

"Today," Father Ignatius began, "I received a request from a Doctor to visit a lady who is one of his patients, and who is very ill."

He spoke seriously, and as if he was choosing every word with care he went on:

"She lives in one of the fine Villas overlooking the bay, and when I saw her, she requested me to find her an Englishwoman who would take her child, a little girl, back to England."

Atayla, who had been leaning back in the bamboo chair in which she had seated herself, sat upright.

She could hardly believe she had heard what the Priest was saying, and it seemed already as if she saw a light at the end of a dark tunnel.

"This lady was very insistent," Father Ignatius went on, "that the person who should escort her child should be an Englishwoman, and as I talked to her I thought of you, realising that this could be the answer to your problem. It would enable you to return to your own country without it costing you anything."

Atayla drew in her breath.

"Father Ignatius, that is exactly what I want! How wonderful that you should have had such a request at this very moment!"

The Priest did not speak, and after a moment Atayla asked:

"What is worrying you? Why are you not pleased by the idea?"

Again Father Ignatius seemed to be feeling for words. Then he said:

"The lady in question calls herself the '*Comtesse* de Soisson,' but she was honest with me, although actually I was already aware of her circumstances. She is not, in fact, married to the *Comte* de Soisson, with whom she is living."

Atayla drew in her breath again.

She was aware that there were many people in Tangiers who were not accepted by the Spanish, who dominated the social life of the town.

People of other nationalities, for personal reasons, made Tangiers their home because they found it convenient to live as they wished without incurring too much censure and condemnation.

There was a pause before she said:

"Is the lady's child, who is to return to England, English or French?"

"It is a little girl, and she is English."

"Then I shall be very willing to take her."

"I thought that was what you would say," Father Ignatius said. "At the same time, it is not right that you should come in contact with a woman who in the eyes of God and His Church is living a life of sin."

"Is this lady a Catholic?"

Father Ignatius shook his head

"No, but the *Comte* is, and he has left his wife and family in France."

The way the Priest spoke told Atayla how deeply he deprecated such behaviour, but she could not help feeling that from her own point of view it was unimportant.

All that mattered was that she could take the lady's daughter back to England, which at least would be the first step in planning to fend for herself.

Because she thought the Priest was hesitating as to whether he would allow her to do such a thing, she bent forward to say eagerly:

"Please, Father, you must realise what this opportunity will mean to me. I have no other way of getting to England, unless I can find work of some sort in Tangiers. Even then it would take me a very long time to save up enough money for my fare, and I have nowhere to stay while I am working."

She saw the Priest's lips move to say that she could stay here with him, but it was quite unnecessary for either of them to say aloud what opposition there would be to this from Mrs. Mansur.

Father Ignatius was too astute and too used to dealing with every type and condition of person not to realise how deeply his Housekeeper resented Atayla being in the Mission.

Her antagonism seemed to vibrate through the small rooms, making not only Atayla but Father Ignatius himself feel that every word Mrs. Mansur uttered was like an unsheathed sword.

"Please, Father," Atayla pleaded. "Let me go and

see this lady and tell her that I am willing to do what she wishes."

The Priest's lips tightened, then he said:

"I have prayed, Atayla. I have prayed all the time I was returning home that I should do the right thing. You are too young to come in contact with such wickedness, and yet, what is the alternative?"

"I promise you, Father, that this wickedness, as you call it, will not affect me. I shall be concerned only with the child, and when she and I leave Tangiers, she will be free of any bad influence her mother might have over her."

As she spoke, Atayla thought that the worry in the Priest's eyes cleared a little. Then he said:

"Now that your father and mother are with God, I feel that the responsibility for what you should do rests with me. That is why I am afraid for you, and yet I am aware that we are all in the hands of a Power greater than ourselves."

"I believe that too," Atayla said. "But you must be aware, Father, that because Papa and I went to such very strange places, and met tribes with many strange customs, I am not ignorant of life and people as I would be if I had just been brought up quietly in England."

This time the Priest smiled.

"I suppose that is true, and, as you say, the customs of some of the tribes would certainly shock many English people if they were aware of them."

"Therefore, Father," Atayla said quickly, "perhaps it is God's will that I should have this chance to get to England, and I am sure that the child's relatives who will welcome her back live exemplary lives!"

The Priest sighed. Then, as if he was aware of Atayla's eagerness and there seemed to be no alternative, he said:

"Go and rest, my child, and when it is cooler I will take you to meet this lady. It is quite a walk and you must not overtire yourself after being so ill."

Atayla knew she had won, and her eyes lit up as she said:

"Thank you, thank you, Father! I feel sure you will never regret allowing me to do this, and I am more grateful than I can say that in this way I can reach England without worrying about how I can find the money."

The Priest did not speak, and Atayla sensed that he was praying he had made the right decision.

She went from the room, closing the door quietly behind her, and went up to her small bedroom, which was very hot at this time of the day.

She lay down on her bed, thinking that once again, as her father would have said, something had "turned up."

That there were difficulties and everything was not plain sailing was unimportant beside the fact that this was the means by which she could reach England.

She hoped that wherever she had to take the child, it would be somewhere in the North, from where she would have a shorter journey to Baronswell, where her father's family house was situated.

Because he had been so obsessed by his work in Africa, her father had very seldom talked of his life as a boy or of his family.

It was her mother who had described to Atayla the large grey brick house standing in its own grounds where her father had been born, and where she had been taken when they became engaged to meet his father and mother.

"They were rather awe-inspiring," her mother had said, "and Papa's brother disapproved of the marriage because he said we could not afford it."

Her mother had laughed as she had added:

"I think they were in fact very surprised that I had agreed to marry your father, and my own family were furious, having expected me to make a very much more advantageous match from a social point of view."

"Is that because you were so pretty, Mama?" Atayla had asked.

"Your father thought I was beautiful," her mother replied. "My father, who was a Baronet, was very proud of his family-tree, and as I was his only child and he was bitterly disappointed not to have a son, he expected great things of me."

"He did not approve of Papa?"

"He thought him delightful—how could he fail to do that?" her mother replied loyally. "But he had no money and was determined to go to Africa, and I was equally determined to go with him."

Her mother laughed as she said:

"I might as well have suggested flying to the moon or setting off for the North Pole. They all talked about Africa as if they were not certain such a place existed!"

"But you enjoyed it, Mama?"

"I have loved every moment of being with your father," her mother answered, "and actually I have become as interested as he is in the tribes and their strange evolution from their contacts with other nations."

As her mother spoke, Atayla knew that she was speaking of how the Berbers, with whom her father was particularly concerned, had mingled with their successive conquerors—the Phoenicians, the Romans, the Vandals, and the Arabs.

When her father had taken his family to the Riff mountains, where the majority of the Berbers lived, being known there as the "Rifft," she had begun to understand why he found them so interesting.

Then year after year as she grew older she began to learn the history of the people of North Africa, who seemed more complex and at the same time more fascinating than any others she read about in her history-books.

She followed the invasion of the Arabs who came from Arabia to the "lands of the farthest West" with "a sword in one hand, and a Koran in the other."

She studied the Moors, whose ancestors overran Spain in their endeavour to spread the Islamic faith, and her father taught her the code of that faith, which enabled its followers to decide what was good and noble in man.

There was so much to learn, so much to admire, and if there were aspects of it which seemed bestial and evil, they were not so important as what was good and fine in the peoples who had roamed over the desert for century upon century.

"What does it matter to me if the *Comtesse* is not really a *Comtesse* and is living with a man who has deserted his wife and family?" Atayla asked herself.

Then she knew how horrified Father Ignatius would be at the question.

"Of course it is wrong," she admitted. "At the same time, Papa never passed judgement on anyone unless they committed an act of cruelty. He believed that everybody had to find their own salvation for themselves, and that is what I want to believe too."

To think of her father brought the tears to her eyes and made her realise how much she missed him, and how difficult it would be to face the future without him.

Because she had been so ill when she had been picked up by some kindly travellers and brought unconscious to Father Ignatius in Tangiers, it had been a long time before the loss of her father had had its full impact upon her mind.

In her first moments of consciousness she had shrunk from acknowledging it even to herself because it was too painful to contemplate.

Then as the days went by and the dagger-wound in her body healed, when she realised that she was alone in the world with nobody to turn to or to help and guide her, she wished that the robbers had killed her as they had killed her father.

Then, because she was young and life was an irresistible force, she knew she had to face things as they were and not as she wanted them to be.

She could almost hear her father laughing at her for being a coward and being afraid.

"Do not worry, something will turn up," he was saying, and that was exactly what had happened!

* * *

Walking through the crowded streets with Father Ignatius, Atayla was too used to women in burnouses and yashmaks shuffling along in babouches and men wearing fezes to notice anything but the way Father Ignatius was leading her.

She was aware that they were leaving the flat-topped houses behind and were climbing a small hill behind the town. They had not gone far before he pointed to where there was a large white Villa surrounded by a high wall.

They went a little farther, and now the view over the sea was breathtaking. But the ground beneath their feet was stony, and there were a number of small goats grazing on the tufts of grass and flowers between the stones.

There were trees, the leaves of which were thick and dark in colour, and Atayla thought they were very beautiful silhouetted against the sky.

She wished she could share their loveliness with somebody but realised that the Priest walking beside her was deep in thought, or prayer, his rosary swinging from his waist with each movement of his sandalled feet.

Then in the centre of the wall was a large, imposing gate, and as soon as they approached, it was opened by a servant dressed in spotless white.

Father Ignatius spoke to him in his own language, and Atayla stared at green lawns, fountains, and a profusion of flowers.

Cypress trees, pointing like long fingers towards the sky, seemed completely in keeping with the Oriental architecture of the Villa.

Without speaking, Father Ignatius walked up to the front door, and it in its turn was opened by a smartly dressed servant, and they were shown into a large cool

room from which there was a magnificent view over the
bay.

It was furnished with deep sofas and armchairs that
looked so comfortable that Atayla thought if once she sat
down in one, it would be hard to get up again.

There were plants in china pots, and paintings
which she knew must be of great value, besides some
exquisite pieces of French furniture that were more
beautiful than anything she had ever seen before.

There was a long wait while she and Father Ignatius
sat on the edges of their armchairs in silence, until a
maid came to his side and said something in Spanish.

Father Ignatius frowned. Then he said to Atayla:

"The maid says her mistress is very weak, and it
would be best for her to see you alone. Go with her, my
child."

Atayla was eager to do so, and only as she walked up
the very elegant staircase did she wonder for the first
time what the lady she was about to see would think of
her.

It had never struck her until this moment that while
she might have been very willing to take the so-called
Comtesse's child to England, there was also a decision to
be made by the mother, who might not be impressed by
her appearance.

The clothes she had been wearing when she was
attacked were threadbare, and her blouse had been torn
and stained from the dagger-thrust.

She had therefore been obliged to accept a dress
from a collection of clothes at the Mission sent there
from England by sewing-parties in Cheltenham, Bath,
and other Provincial towns as an act of Charity.

Atayla had realised it was typical that the material
chosen for what were called "the natives" was a coarse
grey cotton of a particularly ugly hue, which looked drab
and very out-of-place in the brilliant sunshine.

Only orphans and the poorest beggars would accept
such hideous garments when instinctively they longed
for the colour which they saw all round them.

The dress was full in places where it should have
been tight, and tight where it should have been full, but

Atayla had improved it by making a belt out of several handkerchiefs and converting one into a small white collar.

Even so, with a black bonnet on her head, she knew how unprepossessing she must look, and she was suddenly afraid that the child's mother would insist on looking for somebody better dressed and perhaps older to be in charge of her daughter.

"I should have thought of it before," Atayla told herself.

Then she realised that even if she had, there would have been little she could do about it.

In any other household there might have been a woman who would have lent her a slightly more attractive outfit to wear than the one she had on, but she well knew that Mrs. Mansur was only too glad if she looked ugly and would not have lifted a finger to lend her so much as a pair of gloves.

The maid had reached the top of the stairs and was opening the door of a room.

Because it seemed to be expected of her, Atayla followed her into it, and saw that she was in one of the most beautiful bedrooms she had ever seen.

There was a bow-window looking out over the garden and to the sea beyond, there were sun-blinds to keep out the glare of the sun, and dominating the room was an enormous bed draped with white curtains which fell from a corona of gold angels suspended from the ceiling.

In the bed, propped against silk pillows trimmed with wide lace, was one of the loveliest women Atayla could imagine.

Because she had become so accustomed to the Arab women with their dark skin, in contrast the woman in the bed was even more sensational.

She had long golden hair the colour of a corn-field, and small classical features. However, she was very thin and pale, and it was obvious that she was delicate, or perhaps very ill.

Her eyes were closed, and her eye-lashes were dark against the pallor of her cheeks, but as the maid approached she looked up, and it was then that Atayla saw that her eyes were the blue of the sea and thought she was like a flower.

"The young lady's here to see you, *Señora*," the maid said, speaking with a broken accent.

"Yes, yes, of course," the lady in the bed said in little more than a whisper.

The maid moved to one side, motioned Atayla to go forward, and placed a chair for her so that she was as near as possible to the lady in the bed.

Then the maid left the room, and after what seemed a long pause the lady said:

"You have come from Father Ignatius?"

"Yes, *Madame*."

"You are English?"

"Yes, *Madame*."

"The Priest tells me your father was a famous writer."

"That is correct, *Madame*."

"And he is dead?"

"Yes, *Madame*."

There was a little silence, as if the lady was making an effort to remember what she had been told. Then she said:

"You are willing, I understand, to go to England."

"Yes, *Madame*."

"And you will take my daughter with you? I want her to go to her father."

"Her . . . father?"

Atayla could not help her voice sounding somewhat surprised.

"Yes, her father," the lady said. "Felicity should be with him. My—the *Comte*—does not want her here."

The way in which she spoke told Atayla more than her words, and she asked:

"How old is your daughter?"

"She is eight," the lady said, "and has been with me here in Tangiers for three years, but now she must go —home."

"Where am I to take her?" Atayla asked.

There was a pause, then almost as if the lady found
it hard to say the words, she replied:

"To Roth Castle. Her father is the Earl of Rothwell,
and she should be with him, where she belongs."

The lady's voice was suddenly hard. Then, as if she
could not help herself, she said:

"I shall miss her! I shall miss her more than I can
say, but I am not well, and if I die, the *Comte* might not
let her go back."

Atayla could not think what to say to this, so she was
silent until the lady went on:

"You must try to make Felicity understand that as
she is English she must live in England. It will not be
easy for her to return to a life she has forgotten, so you
must help her. Promise me you will help her."

"Of course I will," Atayla replied. "I will do everything I can."

"It will be hard for her, very hard, but there is
nothing else I can do. I know that she will be forgiven
and accepted, while I am damned forever!"

She spoke bitterly, and Atayla knew perceptively
that she did not mean religiously but socially.

Then the lady went on:

"You must take her at once, before the *Comte*
returns. He might try to stop her, and that would make
things more difficult than they are already."

Atayla's eyes widened but she thought she should
not ask questions, but merely take her orders.

The lady was silent for a moment. Then she said:

"I will give you money. It will be expensive to travel
to England, and you must also have a salary."

Atayla was just about to say that she wanted nothing
but her own fare. Then, seeing the beauty and luxury of
the bedroom she was in, she thought she would be very
silly if she did not accept what she was offered.

Somehow it went against her instincts, although she
told herself she must be practical since she owned
nothing and there were things she would need for the
voyage.

"Thank you, *Madame*," she said aloud. "As I expect Father Ignatius told you, my father was killed by desert robbers, who also took literally everything we possessed. So if I am to travel to England with your daughter, I shall have to buy myself a few clothes."

The lady's eyes opened and she said:

"Clothes? But that will take time, and I want you to go at once, tomorrow, if possible."

"I am sure I could find the things I need in the Market," Atayla suggested vaguely.

"No, that is ridiculous!" the lady said. "I have clothes, masses of clothes, and as you are very slim I am sure mine will fit you."

She did not wait for Atayla to reply but reached out and picked up a little gold bell which stood on the table by her bed.

She rang it, and instantly, almost as if she had been listening outside the door, the Spanish maid came in.

"Listen, Mala," the lady said, "I have a trunk filled with clothes that have never been unpacked, since it was too hot to wear them here."

"*Si, señora.*"

"Have it brought downstairs and put in a carriage, and pack another trunk with all the things I do not need any more. There are some coming from Paris this week, and some which arrived last week. The rest I have finished with. Do you understand?"

"*Si, Señora.*"

"Then pack them, pack them quickly! They can go first thing tomorrow morning, or better still the carriage can go into Tangiers tonight and take them to this young lady at the Mission."

"Shall I pack some hats and bonnets, *Señora?*"

"Pack everything. This lady has no clothes at all. They were all stolen from her. She will require to be dressed from her head to her feet. Is that understood?"

"*Si, Señora.*"

"I have far too many clothes, and it is a good

opportunity to dispose of them. Get the other maids to help you. There is no time to be lost!"

"But . . . *Madame* . . ." Atayla expostulated, "it is too much! I cannot possibly accept so many things."

"Do not be foolish," the lady said. "You need them and I have finished with them, and there is no time, I tell you, no time for you to buy anything."

She paused before she continued:

"Now that I think of it, I am making a mistake: you will take Felicity with you now—yes—that would be best—and the trunks will follow as soon as Mala has packed them."

As she spoke she rang the bell again in a feverish manner, and as the maid came hurrying back into the room, she said:

"Fetch Lady Felicity. Tell her I want her, and see that her clothes are packed too, every one of them, you understand? Everything! Her toys, her dolls—everything she possesses!"

The lady spoke in a feverish, almost hysterical manner, and the maid rushed from the room. As soon as she had gone, the lady said, as if she was still making an effort to think of everything:

"I must give you some money!"

There was a little handbag lying on the bed beside her, and she opened it and took out a key.

"The safe is over there," she said, "on the floor under that table."

A little bewildered, Atayla took the key from her, and crossing the room, she saw that there was a large table covered by a cloth, to which the lady was pointing.

For a moment she thought she must be mistaken, then she told herself she should try to be intelligent about this, and raising the cloth she saw that underneath was a large, square safe.

She inserted the key into the lock, pressed down on the handle, and the safe door opened.

"There is a tray on the top shelf," the voice from the bed said, "bring it to me."

Atayla did as she was told, and saw that on the tray were packets of Moroccan francs done up with elastic-bands, and also two brown envelopes like those used in Banks which she was sure contained coins.

"I think I can give you about three hundred pounds," the lady said. "I have no more at the moment, but that will cover the cost of your fare and Felicity's. What is left over you may keep."

"I am sure it is too much," Atayla expostulated.

"I trust you, and I know you are honest. My child must travel First Class in reserved carriages, and in the best cabins of the ships. The train will take you to the halt near Roth Castle in Yorkshire, and from there you must hire a carriage for the last three miles. I trust you to do what is right."

"I promise you I will do exactly what you have told me," Atayla replied.

The lady handed her the rolls of notes and two little brown envelopes, which were very heavy. Atayla held them in her hand, wondering what she should do with them, until the lady said:

"Of course, you have no handbag! There is one of mine in the chest-of-drawers over there. I will give it to you."

Even while she thought this could not be happening, Atayla went to the chest-of-drawers and took out a leather handbag which appeared to her to be very expensive and much finer than anything she had ever owned before.

She took it back to the bed, put the money inside it, and then on the lady's instructions put the tray back in the safe, locked it, and gave her back the key.

As she did so, the door opened, and without anybody announcing her a small girl came into the room.

One glance at her showed Atayla that she was not like her mother, except that her eyes were blue. Otherwise, her face was a different shape, her hair, which was thick and curly, was dark, and she was not delicately made, but rather sturdy.

She ran across the room eagerly, her expensive white dress of muslin and lace showing her bare, dimpled knees, white silk socks, and pretty buttoned shoes.

"Mama, Mama! You are better? Come and play in the garden with me."

"I cannot do that, dearest," her mother said, "and listen, Felicity, I have something to tell you."

"I have a lot to tell you, Mama. I rode my pony today and went very fast."

The lady held Felicity's hand in hers as she said:

"Sit on the bed, my precious, and listen carefully to what I have to tell you. You are going to England!"

"To England, Mama?"

"Yes, dearest, to your father."

"I do not want to go to Papa," Felicity said. "I want to stay here with you. England is cold and foggy, and *Mon Père* says it is not a nice place. He says he hates English people, and it is a pity I am not French."

"You are English, Felicity, and I want you to go to England and see it for yourself. This kind lady is going to take you there. Think how exciting it will be to travel in a big ship and by train."

Felicity put her head on one side and contemplated the idea. Then she asked:

"Can my pony come with me?"

"No, dearest, but your father has dozens of horses, and I am sure he will give you a pony as soon as you arrive."

"I love the pony I have here," Felicity said, "and *Mon Père* says that England is a bad place! Before he went away I knew he was cross with me, because he said I was behaving like an English girl."

The lady looked at Atayla, and she knew she was telling her without words what the *Comte* felt about Felicity.

She was sure he was finding her an encumbrance, and it was tiresome for him to have her in the house where he had installed her mother as his mistress.

It was almost as if somebody were relating a story to her. Atayla could understand that the *Comte* at times missed his own children and found it intolerable to have instead the child of an Englishman whom he disliked.

"What I want you to do now, Felicity darling," the lady said, "is to go and choose all the toys you want to go with you to England—your dolls and, of course, your Teddy Bear!"

She grasped her daughter's small hand in hers and went on:

"Help the maids to pack them carefully so that they are not uncomfortable on the journey, and I know they will find it very exciting to see the great big Castle in which your father lives."

Felicity looked indecisive, and her mother said:

"Go quickly, or they might be forgotten!"

The child gave a little cry, as if the idea frightened her, and without saying any more she jumped down from the bed and ran from the room.

Her mother looked at Atayla, who said:

"She is very attractive, and I am sure you will miss her very much."

"It will break my heart to part with her," the lady said, "but there is nothing I can do but send her away. The *Comte* does not really like her, and she is making things difficult for both of us. Besides, I realise there is no life for her here. When she grows older she must, as her father's daughter, take her proper place in Society."

"That is a long time ahead," Atayla said with a smile.

"She is beginning to notice things," the lady explained, almost as if she spoke to herself. "Yesterday she asked me why she had two fathers, Papa, whom she hardly remembers, and *Mon Père*, who lives with me here. What am I to tell her?"

"I know I seem rather stupid," Atayla said, "but I must get this straight. If your husband is the Earl of Rothwell, then you are the Countess of Rothwell!"

The lady nodded.

"But because it makes the *Comte* happy, I call

myself 'La Comtesse de Soisson,' and that is how I wish to be known by you and everyone. I am sorry you cannot meet him, because he is very, very charming, but his dislike of Felicity is increasing. If I live, it will be a mistake for her to be here, and if I . . . die . . ."

She ceased speaking, and there was a pause.

"I will take Felicity to England," Atayla said. "As you have said, it is where she belongs."

"Thank you."

The lady looked at Atayla as if she saw her for the first time and said:

"You are very pretty, and when you are well dressed you will look prettier still. Let me beg you—do not listen to your heart. If you do—then you will do mad, crazy things—as I have done—and once you have thrown your bonnet over the wind-mill, there is no going back!"

Chapter Two

When they left the Mission the next morning, Atayla could hardly believe it was really happening.

She supposed it was because she was still weak from her wound and the fever which had followed it that she found it difficult to grasp that so much was taking place so quickly.

And yet, she had thought afterwards that while she was in the Villa she had been quite efficient.

After the *Comtesse* had given her orders for the packing to be done and Felicity had left them, Atayla had said hesitatingly:

"I think, *Madame,* I should go downstairs and tell Father Ignatius that I am to leave him tomorrow, and also that Lady Felicity will come back with me tonight to the Mission."

"Yes, of course," the *Comtesse* agreed, "and while you are away I will try to think of anything else you will need."

"Thank you," Atayla said.

She hurried from the room and down the curved white staircase to where Father Ignatius was sitting where she had left him.

He had obviously been looked after, for in front of him was a glass of the mint tea which every guest in Morocco is offered whether it is a private house he enters or a shop.

With it were the traditional sweetmeats, mostly of almonds and honey, and little cakes made with coconut.

As Atayla joined him, the servant who had let them in immediately brought her a glass of mint tea, and because she felt she needed sustenance she sipped it gratefully.

"Eat, my child," Father Ignatius said, pushing a plate of sweetmeats towards her, and after the very inadequate meal she had cooked for herself in the Mission, Atayla reached out towards them eagerly.

"There is so much I have to tell you," she said when she could get her breath, "and I hardly know where to begin."

Father Ignatius smiled.

"I imagine the *Comtesse* has asked you to leave as soon as possible for England with her daughter."

"That is right," Atayla replied.

"I think in case there is any difficulty with which she has not the strength to cope, she is anxious to get her away before the *Comte* returns," the Priest said.

"She wishes us to take Lady Felicity back with us now."

Father Ignatius nodded, as if that was what he had expected, and Atayla had the idea that he knew far more about the situation than he had told her.

"Also," Atayla said a little shyly, "*Madame* has been extremely kind in giving me a great quantity of clothes. I explained to her that all mine had been stolen by the robbers."

"That is generous and makes things much easier for you," Father Ignatius replied. "I am well aware that the clothes you are wearing at the moment would not be suitable for a journey to England or when you present yourself on arrival."

Atayla looked at him in surprise, then realised his eyes were twinkling.

She thought, as had occurred to her before since her arrival at the Mission, that Father Ignatius had a great deal of worldly knowledge in addition to spiritual.

Then she put down the sweetmeat she had been eating and said:

"I have just thought . . . the maids are packing the clothes the *Comtesse* has given me, but I shall have no time to unpack them and find something to wear for the journey. Shall I go ask the maid if she will kindly put out what I will need in a separate case?"

"That certainly seems a sensible thing to do," Father Ignatius replied.

Atayla rose to her feet and walked up the staircase again, hoping she would find Mala, the maid, without having to ask the *Comtesse* where she was.

When she reached the landing she heard voices, and two doors away from the *Comtesse's* room she found Mala and three other maids busily taking gowns from several built-in wardrobes and packing them into large leather trunks.

Atayla could not believe they were all for her, but the maids looked up when she appeared and Mala said:

"You want me, *Señorita?*"

"Yes," Atayla replied. "I came to ask you if you would be very kind and put a gown and coat in which I could travel in a separate case from the other things. If the trunks are to arrive at the Mission tonight, there will be no time in which to unpack anything."

"*Si, si, Señorita,* I should have thought of it," Mala said crossly, as if her efficiency as a lady's-maid was in question.

She spoke quickly in Spanish to the other maids. Then to Atayla:

"Do not worry, *Señorita,* it will be arranged, and as you have nothing of your own, I will pack separately everything for the voyage so that you need not open the other trunks until after you reach your destination."

"Thank you very much," Atayla said. "It is very kind of you."

As she turned away, the maid gave a little cry.

"Wait, *Señorita,* wait!" she said. "There is the

problem of shoes. Try on a pair belonging to the *Señora* and see if they fit you."

She snapped her fingers, and one of the other maids brought from the wardrobe a pair of very elegant kid shoes that were smarter than anything Atayla had ever seen, let alone owned.

She pulled off the worn, flat-heeled black leather shoes which were all the Mission could offer, and slipped her feet into the *Comtesse*'s.

They seemed a trifle tight, but that, she thought, was very likely owing to the fact that she had been wearing loose shoes, and also it was very hot.

Mala held up her hands in delight.

"That makes everything easy," she said. "I was afraid the *Señorita* would look very elegant on top, but have to go barefoot, as the *Señora* has very small feet."

"These are very lovely," Atayla said. "Thank you again for all you are doing for me."

She thought the maids seemed pleased by her gratitude. Then, feeling embarrassed at being given so much, she hurried down the stairs again to Father Ignatius.

"I have been thinking," he said as she sat down, "that if the *Comtesse* wishes to leave tomorrow, you will have to take the ship to Gibraltar. It leaves early and takes four hours for the crossing."

"The *Comtesse* insists that Lady Felicity has a cabin on every ship in which we travel, and a reserved First Class carriage on every train."

"I will see what I can do about that," Father Ignatius promised. "I hope she has given you enough money for such extravagances."

"She has been very generous."

"You will find it expensive," the Priest said, "and you will doubtless have to stay in London before you can catch a train to the North."

Atayla looked worried.

"When I last stayed in London," she said, "it was

with Mama and Papa in a private house. I do not know of
an Hotel where I could take Lady Felicity."

"Leave this to me," Father Ignatius said. "I have a
friend who deals with travellers who come to Tangiers
and arranges their transport not only in Morocco but also
in Europe."

Atayla gave a little sigh of relief and said:

"I have travelled so much with Papa that it should
hold no fears for me. But, as you know, Father, I am
more used to camels than trains, and dhows than
steamships!"

Father Ignatius laughed.

"That is true, but you are a sensible girl, and I am
sure you will soon adjust yourself to the difference."

"I hope so," Atayla said.

It had of course always been her father who had
arranged the caravans in which they crossed the desert,
and when they were not sleeping in their own tents,
there was usually not much choice when it came to
Hotels in native towns.

It was not until they were driving back in the
Comte's comfortable carriage that Atayla felt exhausted,
and also apprehensive of what lay ahead.

There had been an emotional scene when the
Comtesse had said good-bye to her daughter, and because she had wept and kissed the little girl over and
over again, Felicity had cried too.

"You will not forget me, my darling, promise me
you will not forget me," the *Comtesse* pleaded.

Even with the tears running down her cheeks and
her blue eyes wet with them she still looked exceedingly
beautiful.

But when Atayla finally took Felicity by the hand
and drew her toward the door, she looked back to see
the *Comtesse* lying with closed eyes against the pillows
and seemingly on the point of collapse.

"I do not . . . want to leave . . . Mama," Felicity
wept. "I want to . . . stay here with my . . . pony."

"You will have a pony in England," Atayla prom-

ised, "and think how exciting it will be tomorrow to go in
a big ship on the sea!"

However, Felicity was not appeased, and all the
way from the Villa to the Mission she cried and said she
wished to stay with her mother.

Atayla thought wearily that they would doubtless go
from one emotional upset to another, and Mrs. Mansur
would be annoyed that Father Ignatius had brought
another guest to stay at the Mission.

But Mrs. Mansur was so delighted to hear that
Atayla was leaving the next morning that she hurriedly
prepared a bed for Felicity, and the supper was more
palatable than anything Atayla had eaten since she had
become well enough to notice the food.

They had driven back without any luggage, as Mala
had said it was not yet ready, and there was a great deal
more packing yet to be done.

There was no sign of it when the evening meal was
finished, and as Atayla rose from the table she was
wondering what Felicity would think of having to go to
bed in a shapeless, thick calico nightgown which was all
that was obtainable at the Mission, when there was a
knock on the door.

Mrs. Mansur went to open it and they heard her
voice scream shrilly at what she saw outside.

Atayla looked across the table at Father Ignatius.

"I expect the luggage has arrived."

There was a faint smile on his lips as he replied:

"I am sure Mrs. Mansur will find it somewhat
overwhelming. Take the child upstairs while I cope with
it."

Atayla obeyed him, and as they went up the small,
rickety staircase, she saw the *Comtesse*'s servants carrying in a number of huge leather trunks and thought they
would be another responsibility for her on the voyage.

She had not been mistaken in this, for the next
morning, after a restless night in which she found it
difficult to sleep, she had gone downstairs to be appalled
at the mountain of baggage.

It filled the small entrance-hall and spilt over into what was the Waiting-Room for those who wished to have an interview with Father Ignatius.

The leather trunks were all obviously expensive ones, some with carved tops, some with heavy straps.

There were also a number of hat-boxes, which Atayla looked at longingly, then she searched for the case in which Mala had promised to pack her clothes for the voyage.

She was far too nervous to ask Mrs. Mansur to have it brought up to her, so on rising she had put on her usual shapeless grey cotton gown.

Now she saw that there was in fact a smaller trunk, a very elegant one bearing an embossed coronet.

She knew instinctively that it was English and must have been part of the luggage which the *Comtesse* had brought with her when she left the Earl of Rothwell.

Atayla pulled it away from the heap of baggage and was just wondering how she was to get it upstairs, when one of the younger Priests who worked with Father Ignatius came from the Study.

He was a very earnest young man, of French nationality, and Atayla had the idea that whenever he saw her he looked the other way in case she should prove a temptation to him.

Then, before he could slip through the outside door, she said quickly:

"I wonder if you would be very kind and carry this trunk upstairs? I am afraid it is too heavy for me to manage alone, and I do not want to worry Father Ignatius if I can help it."

"No, of course not," the young Priest replied.

He lifted up the small trunk without any difficulty and hurried up the stairs, almost, Atayla thought with a faint smile, as if the Devil was at his heels.

She had already noticed that there was a label on the trunk on which was written FOR THE JOURNEY, and now she saw a similar label was attached to one of the small hat-boxes.

Carrying it in her hand, she climbed the stairs after the Priest.

He had already placed the trunk in her bedroom, and as he came from it he did not look at her but hurried down the stairs, and had almost reached the front door before she could thank him.

"Thank you, thank you!" she called.

He murmured something in too low a voice for her to hear it, then the Mission door slammed shut behind him.

Atayla laughed because it was difficult to believe she could be a temptation to anybody, looking as she did in the hideous gray cotton gown.

Then, excited as she had not been since her father died, she undid the straps of the small trunk and threw back the lid.

Five minutes later she looked at herself in the mirror and gasped. She could hardly believe she was the same person who had walked up to the Villa yesterday with Father Ignatius.

The *Comtesse*'s gown fitted her almost as if it had been made for her, and it was so exquisite and so elegant that Atayla felt that any woman seeing it would know that it came from Paris.

Of blue silk, the colour of the *Comtesse*'s eyes, it had a neat little jacket ending at the waist to wear over it, and although she could hardly believe it, as she took it from the trunk she found a cape in the same material edged with sable that reached from her neck to the ground.

"How could she possibly part with anything so expensive?" Atayla questioned.

Then as she delved deeper into the trunk she found underclothes trimmed with lace that were more beautiful than anything she had ever imagined she might see, let alone own.

There was a silk petticoat that rustled like the wind in the trees when she put it on, there was a nightgown and a negligé, slippers trimmed with marabou, and quite a number of other small items that she had no time to inspect.

She was aware that time was passing and she must wake Felicity and get her dressed for the journey.

Felicity's travelling-case had been brought up to her room last night by Father Ignatius, and Atayla had appreciated that the nightgown and the pretty little dressing-gown trimmed with lace was laid on the top.

Beneath these was a coat that matched the dress the child had worn when she left the Villa and in which she was obviously intended to travel the next day.

Atayla then opened the hat-box and found a small, pretty toque in the same colour as her gown, trimmed only with veiling.

However, it was so smart that she felt despairingly that her hair was not worthy of such a crown to embellish it.

Hastily she brushed it back from her forehead, and coiled it at the back of her head in a more elegant chignon than she usually wore.

It did not seem to Atayla from what she could remember a very fashionable coiffure, and it was to be a long time before she realised that across the Atlantic, Dana Gibson had introduced a new look for the American woman, which had also become the rage of England and France.

Anyway, as she looked at herself in the mirror she could not help feeling that she was viewing a complete stranger, somebody she had never met before, and who not only looked what her mother would have called a "Lady" but also was undoubtedly extremely attractive.

Then, because she knew she was loitering when she should be busy, Atayla hurried into the next room to wake Felicity.

* * *

They drove through the crowded streets down to the Quay with two hired carriages because it was impossible to get all the luggage into one.

A great number of people stared at them because

vehicles on wheels were few and far between in Tangiers.

Atayla suddenly felt that she could not leave the land she knew so well and in which she had spent so many years of her life.

What did she know of England? She was familiar only with the desert and the tribes who roamed and lived in it.

The cities of Morocco, which her father had said with their packed streets and fortified walls, with gates which were shut at night, were more mediaeval than anything to be found in more civilised parts of the world.

"I shall be alien to everything in England, and I had much better stay here," Atayla told herself.

Then she remembered the hostility she had encountered from Mrs. Mansur and knew that without her father neither Morocco nor any other part of North Africa would welcome her as an unattached and unprotected woman, nor was there any work for her because she was so young.

'I am a Nomad, a wanderer without roots,' she thought a little bitterly.

Then she was ashamed because she knew she should be grateful that something had turned up at the last moment, when she had no money and little chance of earning any.

She put out her hand towards Father Ignatius.

"I want to thank you, Father," she said, "not only for your great kindness in nursing me back to health but for letting me stay with you, and of course for finding a very comfortable way for me to return to England."

"God answered my prayers," Father Ignatius said simply. "I know, my child, that it was meant that you should go back to your father's and mother's country, which is also yours, even though it may seem strange to you at first."

Atayla felt he had read her thoughts and been aware of the fear she was trying to hide from him.

'If the worst comes to the worst,' she thought, 'I can come back.'

At the same time, she knew that would not be a very practical move, and she would somehow have to adjust herself to England and to her father's relatives, if she could find them.

Then there was the bustle and the excitement of going aboard the ship, and because it was very crowded, it was a relief to find that Father Ignatius's friend had procured a private cabin for them.

He also had their First Class tickets for the train which would carry them from Gibraltar to Madrid, and from Madrid to Calais.

"You will have to change at Madrid," he told Atayla, "but when you get there go at once to the Ticket Office and ask them not only the times of the trains but for a reserved carriage, and they will advise you which is the quickest and best way to reach England."

"Thank you, I will do that," Atayla answered.

"It may mean," he went on, "taking a ship from Le Havre rather than Calais, but I do not have enough information here to help you."

Atayla thanked him again. At the same time, she hoped rather doubtfully that it would be as easy as he made it sound.

Then she told herself she was being ridiculous. If she and her father could find their way over miles and miles of sandy desert without getting lost, there was no reason why she should lose herself and Felicity when it was really a straightforward journey across Europe.

At the same time, it was hard to say good-bye to Father Ignatius.

He seemed to be her last contact with her old life, and she was setting out alone on an uncharted course without a guide and without even a compass.

"May God bless you, my child," Father Ignatius said, "and keep you safe. If you are in any difficulty, pray, and help will always come to you."

Then he had gone ashore, and Atayla and Felicity

waved good-bye as the ship's engines began to turn, and
they moved slowly away from the Quay.

Felicity wanted to run round the deck, but there
were too many people crowded on it, and Atayla persuaded her to come into the cabin.

"We have a little house all to ourselves," she said.
"Let us sit down and make ourselves comfortable, and if
you would like something to eat or drink, I am sure I can
find a steward to bring it to you."

The child was at first restless, then Atayla told her a
story in which a dhow that she and her father were
travelling in became becalmed in the centre of a huge
lake and they did not know how they were to reach the
shore.

Felicity listened, then asked for another story.
Atayla soon found that she was insatiable in her demands
for them.

Although it was an excellent way of keeping her
amused and quiet on what was to prove a very long and
arduous journey, she herself became tired of her own
voice, and longed to sleep, or at least to be able to think
quietly.

The only thing, she knew later, which saved her
from collapsing was the food she was able to buy at the
different stations, and which, after the meagre fare
provided by Mrs. Mansur, seemed delicious and was
certainly sustaining.

As they passed through Spain there was plenty of
fresh fruit to be bought, and when they crossed the
frontier into France there were pies and pastries that
were different from anything Atayla had eaten for a long
time.

Felicity was, she discovered, an intelligent little girl
who had moments of shewdness that made her seem
older than her age.

Soon after they started, she said to Atayla:

"When *Mon Père* comes home he'll be surprised to
find me gone."

"I am sure he will," Atayla replied.

"He'll also be glad," Felicity said. "He does not like me. Why does he not like me?"

"I am sure you are mistaken," Atayla said quickly. "He loves you, but sometimes he had to reprove you if you did anything wrong."

Felicity shook her head, making her dark curls dance round her cheeks.

"No, he does not like me," she said, "and Mala says it is because he hates my Papa."

Atayla did not know what to say, and after a moment Felicity went on:

"I have two fathers! Most girls have only one father, but I have two."

"Then you are very lucky. My father is dead, so I have no father and I miss him very much."

Felicity's attention was diverted from herself.

"Why did your father die?"

Atayla told her the story of how they had been set upon by robbers in the desert, and the child listened with fascination.

"And they tried to kill you too?" she asked.

Atayla nodded.

"They thought I was dead," she said, "but God kept me alive, perhaps so that I should be useful in taking you to England."

Felicity pondered over this for a moment or two. Then she said:

"It seems a funny way to choose me a Governess. Mama says you're to be my Governess and teach me lots of things about England."

"That is what I hope to do," Atayla said, "but as I have not been to England for some time, perhaps you will have to teach me!"

Felicity laughed.

"I remember lots of things about England, so I will be able to teach you."

When they reached Calais, Atayla felt they had been travelling for weeks, because there had been a long wait for a train at Madrid.

As they had arrived late at night and would be leaving early in the morning, it was not worth going to an Hotel, and they had therefore slept rather uncomfortably in the Ladies' Waiting-Room.

Atayla's insistence on having reserved carriages ensured that they were treated with respect, and also, she thought, with some amusement at their impressive mountain of luggage.

Everywhere they changed there were a number of porters only too willing to carry it because it looked expensive.

The Channel crossing was fortunately fairly smooth, certainly not half as rough, Atayla thought with a smile, as riding on the back of a camel.

However, she persuaded Felicity to lie down in the cabin in case she felt sick, and to her relief the child fell asleep.

Then there was a long train journey to London, and when they arrived, as Atayla had expected, they were told they had to change stations for the trains to the North.

As Felicity was tired and hungry, Atayla did not waste time in making enquiries about trains leaving late in the evening, but asked the Station Master, who stood resplendent in a tall hat on the platform, if he could recommend a quiet, respectable Hotel.

One look at the elegant way in which she was dressed made him reply with hardly a pause that he was quite certain she would be comfortable at Brown's Hotel in Dover Street.

Atayla took his advice and drove there, but when she received the bill the next morning she was horrified at how expensive it was.

The large tip she was obliged to give and the extravagant way they were travelling were fast swallowing up the money the *Comtesse* had given her.

She had also learnt that the Moroccan francs were priced very low against European currency.

However, she was confident that she had enough to

reach Roth Castle, but it was obvious that there would
be very little left over, and when the journey was
finished she would be as penniless as she had been
before it had begun.

But after a good and substantial breakfast at Brown's
Hotel, she did not feel worried, and accepted the
Manager's suggestion that as they had a long journey in
front of them they should take a packed luncheon from
the Hotel for the train, and augment it on the journey
with hampers which would be supplied at the main
stations at which they stopped.

It all sounded so comfortable that Atayla agreed
instantly. At the same time, she was aware that this was
yet another drain on the money in her handbag, which
was dwindling away day by day.

The Manager of Brown's sent with them to the train
a Commissionaire who obtained their reserved carriage
for them and ordered their hampers, and of course he
too had to be generously tipped.

When the train moved off, Felicity said:

"I'm tired of travelling. I want to ride my pony in
the sunshine!"

Atayla thought that was what she too would like, but
there was no sunshine, only dark clouds and scuds of
rain which splattered against the window.

She remembered learning:

> *March winds and April showers*
> *Bring forth May flowers.*

It was not yet May and she was sure that April in
England was really unpredictable, despite Browning's
eulogy about it.

Ever since they had left Gibraltar she had been glad
of her travelling-cloak, although every time she put it on
she could hardly believe that she, Atayla, was wearing
anything trimmed with sable.

She was certain it must have cost more money than
her father could ever have earned from his writing.

Felicity's cloak was warmly lined and the collar and

cuffs were of velvet. There was, however, in the bottom of her case a small tippet of white ermine with little black tails, and a muff to match.

When Atayla produced it, Felicity had exclaimed:

"I had that years and years ago when I was very little, but I have not wanted them in Tangiers."

"No, of course not," Atayla agreed, "it was much too hot. But you will find they will keep your fingers nice and warm in England, where it can be cold even in the spring."

"Is that what it is now?" Felicity enquired. "*Mon Père* is right, it is dull and ugly, and I want to go home!"

Atayla thought that was what she would like too, but there was no point in saying so, and she merely tried to divert Felicity's attention to something else.

As they were in the Edinburgh Express, Atayla had learnt that they should reach the Halt for Roth Castle at about five o'clock in the evening.

However, this proved to be optimistic, for there were delays at two stations, and later when she asked the time she found the train was already an hour late.

It was no use complaining, and time seemed to drag by until finally when it was long after six o'clock the train came to a standstill at a very small platform on which was a Notice Board saying: HALT FOR ROTH CASTLE

The Guard came hurrying to the door of the carriage and helped them to alight, and when they had done so the train had to move on quite a considerable way so that the van which contained their luggage was at the platform.

There was only one old Porter and he seemed to Atayla to take an endless time to get all their trunks out, and when finally this was achieved the old man stared at them helplessly.

"Ye goin' t' the Castle, Lady?" he asked Atayla. "There b'aint a carriage to meet ye."

"I would like to hire one," Atayla said.

The Porter pushed his cap back and scratched his head.

"It be too late fer that," he said, "an' we was given no instructions there was visitors arrivin'."

"We have to get there," Atayla said a little desperately, "and this little girl is very tired. It has been a long journey."

"'Is Lordship be expectin' ye?"

It was a question she had not anticipated, and because she thought it would be a mistake to say "no," Atayla replied:

"I hope so, unless the post has delayed my letter, which might have happened."

This seemed quite reasonable, and Atayla thought the Porter accepted it.

"Weel, sit ye down," he said, "an' Oi'll see wot Oi can do."

"I'm tired," Felicity complained. "I want to see the Castle."

"We just have to wait a little while," Atayla said, "while they find a carriage to take us there."

"Why is there no carriage waiting for us?"

Felicity spoke in an affronted manner, which made Atayla think with a smile that children soon grew used to luxury and took it as their right.

So that they could keep warm and be out of the bitter wind blowing over the countryside, they went into the tiny, box-like Waiting-Room, and Atayla managed to light the fire in the small grate.

There was only a newspaper and a few large sticks of wood with which to do so, but fortunately there was a box of matches on the mantelshelf, and it amused Felicity to watch Atayla getting it going.

Atayla could not help thinking that she was not correctly dressed for such a menial task, and she was very careful not to dirty the beautiful long suede gloves that Mala had put in with her travelling-clothes.

They were already rather creased and did not look as clean as they had when she had started out on the journey, but at least she felt they gave a finish to her whole appearance.

She hoped that in consequence the Earl would approve of her and allow her to remain at least for a little while as Felicity's Governess.

She had thought it over very carefully while they were travelling, and had decided that from her own point of view it would be wise until she could get her bearings to try to convince the Earl that, since she had been engaged as a Governess for Felicity, that was what she should remain.

She could not believe that he would find it easy to get somebody else very quickly.

An added complication was that when she had tipped the Porter and paid for the carriage to the Castle, there would not be much more than a pound or two left from the money the *Comtesse* had given her.

"I must earn something," she told herself firmly. "Then at least I shall be able to leave when I want to."

At the same time, she knew it was an uncomfortable position in which to be, and she only hoped that the Earl would accept her services and give her a generous salary.

The fire was going well and Felicity was warming her hands by it when the Porter returned.

"Oi've found a carriage for ye, Lady," he said, "but 'tis on'y 'cause ye be goin' to the Castle. Oi persuaded Jim Roberts to take ye there. 'E don't turn out as a rule after 'e's stabled 'is 'orse for the night."

"I am very grateful," Atayla said.

She realised that she would have to double what she had intended to give the Porter and was quite certain that Jim Roberts would expect a double fare as well.

When he did arrive, in a very old closed Brougham which smelt of hay, horse, and dry leather, he was appalled at the mountain of luggage.

"Oi can't take all that gear on this!" he said firmly.

"You could make two journeys," Atayla suggested, "and if some of the trunks can be locked up for the night, they can be left until tomorrow morning."

This seemed to appease Jim Roberts slightly, and he

and the Porter piled up quite half of the luggage onto
the front and the back of the Brougham, besides packing
the hat-boxes inside on the small seat opposite Atayla
and Felicity.

When they finally moved off, Atayla was almost
afraid the horses would find it impossible to pull them,
but they managed it, and they left behind only four big
trunks to be collected on the following day.

She was aware as they drove away that dusk was
falling, and Jim Roberts had lit the candle-lanterns on
either side of the carriage.

"Now you are going to show me the Castle, which,
if you remember, I have never seen," Atayla said.

"I have forgotten! I have forgotten what it is like,"
the child replied crossly.

"But you have not forgotten your father?"

Felicity thought for some minutes. Then she said:

"Papa was very cross with Mama. He shouted at her
and she cried."

Atayla was wondering what she should say to this
when Felicity finished:

"Then Mama and I went away to *Mon Père*. He was
very, very glad to see Mama, and he never shouted at
her."

Atayla felt that this was uncomfortably revealing,
and to divert Felicity's attention she said:

"Tell me about the Castle. Is it very old?"

"I'm cold," Felicity said. "I want to go back to the
sun! I want Mama!"

At the warning note that she was about to cry,
Atayla put her arms round her.

"Sit close to me," she said, "and keep warm, and I
will tell you a story about how my father and I once saw a
lake with lots of big crocodiles in it and how frightening
they were."

The story lasted until Atayla was aware that they
were passing through some huge stone-flanked gates
with lodges on either side of them that had cressellated
tops as if they were tiny Castles.

Then there was a long drive which was dark because of the trees on either side of it, and then in the far distance she saw lights which she was sure came from windows.

Suddenly the trees ended and she had her first glimpse of Roth Castle.

It was certainly very impressive, very large, with a huge round tower on one side and turrets that were silhouetted against the sky.

"We are here," Atayla said with a lilt in her voice, "and look how large and exciting your Castle is!"

As they drew nearer she thought perhaps "exciting" was the wrong word, for there was something heavy, dark, and menacing about the Castle that made her feel afraid.

Then she told herself she was being ridiculous; she was over-tired, it was getting late, and no building, however beautiful, looked its best in the dark.

When they drew nearer still, there seemed to be only two windows with any light in them, and just one light in the shape of a lantern over a huge stone Gothic-arched front door.

The tired horses came to a standstill, and Atayla made no effort to move, hoping the servants inside the Castle would be aware that somebody had arrived and the door would open.

But there was no movement, and Jim Roberts got down from the cab and walked slowly and heavily up the steps, stamping his feet as he did so as if they were cold.

He tugged at an iron bell beside the door and waited until what seemed to Atayla a very long time had passed before the door opened.

It was then she decided that it would be wise to alight, and opening the carriage door for herself she said to Felicity:

"Come along, dearest. Now you can go inside and get warm."

She climbed out as she spoke, and taking the child

by the hand walked up the steps to where she saw an elderly Butler standing in the doorway, staring in astonishment at the luggage on the carriage below.

"Is the Earl of Rothwell at home?" Atayla asked.

Even as she asked the question it suddenly struck her how embarrassing it would be if he was away and in his absence the household refused to let them in.

But to her relief the Butler replied:

"His Lordship's in residence, Madam, but I don't think His Lordship's expecting visitors."

"No, but it is of great importance that I should see him," Atayla replied.

"His Lordship'll see you, Madam, only if you've an appoint . . ."

He could not go on, because Atayla interrupted him to say:

"Will you tell His Lordship that I have brought his daughter, Lady Felicity Roth, to him?"

The Butler stared at her, then stared down at Felicity in astonishment, before he said in a different tone:

"Well, Your Ladyship's grown a great deal since I last saw you!"

"I am eight," Felicity announced, "and I remember the flags."

As she spoke she pointed to where over the huge, mediaeval stone fireplace there were ancient flags jutting out from the wall.

"Of course you do," the Butler said. "Your Ladyship always wanted to play with them, but if you touch 'em they'll fall to bits."

"Why will they fall to bits?" Felicity enquired.

"Because they're old, very old, Your Ladyship," the Butler replied.

He looked at Atayla.

"Will you come this way, Madam, and I'll tell His Lordship of your arrival. He'll be surprised, very surprised to see Her Ladyship!"

Atayla did not reply, and the Butler led the way

across the marble Hall, on which were laid some Persian rugs.

He opened a door, and as Atayla went in followed by Felicity he said:

"I'll see to your luggage, Madam. I presume Her Ladyship's staying here?"

"I hope so," Atayla replied. "We have nowhere else to go at this hour of the night."

Then as the Butler would have moved away she said:

"I must pay the cabman."

"Leave that to me, Madam," the Butler answered, and shut the door of the room.

It was a Sitting-Room and there were gas-lights on each side of the mantelpiece and a large oil-lamp on a table that was heaped with books.

As Atayla looked round she realised there were also a number of bookcases and a large, flat-topped writing-desk in front of what when the curtains were opened she was sure was a long window.

There were comfortable sofas and deep armchairs such as a man would enjoy, and as there was a fire burning brightly in the hearth, she was sure that this was the Earl's Private Room, where he sat when he was alone.

"Do you remember this room?" she asked Felicity.

The child was not interested. She had sat down on the sofa and put her head against the cushions.

"I'm tired," she said, "and I'm thirsty!"

"I will ask for a drink as soon as we can go upstairs," Atayla said, "but you must remember we have taken much longer to arrive here than we expected, because the train was delayed, and it may take us a little time to get all the things we want."

"I'm tired," Felicity said again.

She yawned, and because the round hat she wore on the back of her head was obviously making her uncomfortable, Atayla undid the ribbons under her chin and took it away from her.

She fluffed out her hair over her ears and thought she looked very pretty and attractive, and it would be impossible for the Earl not to appreciate his daughter.

Then she wondered a little apprehensively if he would resent their arrival so late at night unannounced and without his having any warning that his wife was returning his child to him.

She had in fact wondered once or twice on the journey if it was a wise thing to do, and she thought she should have asked the *Comtesse* to write to Felicity's father and perhaps explain to him why she could no longer keep the child with her.

But it had seemed not only far too intimate and personal for her to speak in such a way, but also, she thought, it was none of her business.

All she had done was to accept the job of taking Felicity back to the Earl, and there was no reason why she should be involved any deeper in the situation than that.

And yet, she thought a little uncomfortably, she was involved because she was here and the *Comtesse* was far away.

The door opened, and she looked up quickly and apprehensively, but it was only the Butler returning.

"His Lordship's having his dinner, Madam," he said. "When he's finished, I think he'll see you."

He did not wait for Atayla's reply, but closed the door again, and she thought she did not like the sound of "I *think* he will see you."

"What else can he do?" she asked herself.

Felicity was complaining again.

"I'm thirsty. Give me something to drink!"

Atayla looked quickly round the room, thinking perhaps there would be a grog-tray on which she would find some water or lemonade, but there was nothing there.

She was afraid that if she opened the door and looked outside into the Hall for the Butler, she might instead encounter the Earl coming from the Dining-

Room, and he would think she was behaving in a strange manner in his house.

She was sure that the Butler and the footman were in fact waiting on him in the Dining-Room, and that was why there had been a long delay before the door-bell was answered.

"I am sorry, dearest," she said to Felicity. "I cannot get you anything at the moment, but it will not be long now, and we will ask for some nice milk like you had at the Hotel."

She had been amused at how delighted Felicity was with English milk, which was something she had not had in Tangiers and was not even obtainable in France.

Thick and creamy, she had drunk it down with relish and asked for more.

Vaguely Atayla remembered how much she had enjoyed milk when she was very small and when she had stayed in England for her grandfather's Funeral.

But she had grown so used to the lack of it in Africa that she had not missed it until she had tasted it again.

Time passed and she was conscious of the tick of the clock on the mantelpiece. Then as Felicity was very quiet she realised that the child was asleep.

Carefully, so as not to awaken her, she lifted her two little legs in their white socks up onto the sofa, then sat very stiff and still on the edge of it, waiting.

Suddenly the door opened and the Earl came in, and one look at him made her feel apprehensive.

He seemed very tall and overpowering. His hair was dark, as she had somehow expected it would be, like Felicity's.

His eyes were dark too, and he was scowling so deeply that his eye-brows seemed to meet over his straight, aristocratic nose, and as he walked towards her Atayla was aware that his mouth was set in a hard line.

His appearance was so frightening and indeed so awe-inspiring that she rose nervously to her feet, and as he reached her he looked at her, then at the sleeping child, then back at her.

"Who are you?" he asked. "And what the hell are you doing here?"

Chapter Three

The way he spoke, and the manner in which his words appeared to vibrate round the room, took Atayla's voice away.

Then as she remembered that he knew who Felicity was and had been told that they both had arrived, she said quietly:

"I have brought your daughter . . . home."

"On whose instructions?" the Earl enquired. "Or need I ask? Well, you can go back to where you came from!"

Atayla stared at him in sheer astonishment. Then she said, and her voice sounded weak and feeble even to herself:

"That . . . is impossible!"

"Nothing is impossible!" the Earl snapped. "You can tell whoever sent you that I have no intention of accepting any communication from her, except through my Solicitors."

He turned and walked towards the door, and as he reached it he said:

"Get out, and quickly!"

Because it was obvious that he meant to leave the room, Atayla gave a little cry of sheer horror, and moving hastily towards him said:

"You cannot do . . . this! You cannot send us away now . . . at this time of the . . . night!"

"Why not?" the Earl asked. "I did not invite you

here, and I am sure you can find a more appropriate place to stay."

The way he spoke was somehow insulting, but Atayla was too agitated to realise it.

Because she was frightened she pleaded:

"Please . . . we have been travelling for days and I cannot take Felicity . . . out again, even if I had anywhere to take her. She is very . . . tired."

"That is your business!"

"You . . . do not understand," Atayla said. "We have come all the way from Tangiers."

The Earl had once again turned towards the door and his hand was on the handle. Now he looked back.

"Tangiers?" he questioned. "I thought she would be in . . ."

Then he interrupted himself to say again harshly:

"It is none of my business! She has had the child with her for three years and now she can keep her!"

"You cannot say that," Atayla argued. "Felicity was not . . . happy where she . . . was, and her mother was insistent that she should come . . . home where she . . . belongs."

The Earl laughed, and it was a very unpleasant sound.

"Where she belongs! It is a bit late for that now! No! I will not accept the very belated return of what was once mine. Take the child back to her mother and be damned to you!"

Perhaps it was the swear-word more than anything else that made Atayla lose her temper.

She was frightened, at the same time she thought the Earl was being brutal to Felicity, and she hated him for his behaviour and for the cruel way in which he was speaking.

She had no idea how her grey eyes were flashing fire at him as she said:

"Very well, My Lord, if that is your last word, Felicity and I will leave. But as we have nowhere to go, we can perhaps sleep on your doorstep, or shelter in one

of your barns for the night, as there could be no other
accommodation for us at this late hour."

As she was speaking to him no less angrily than he
had, the Earl seemed for the moment somewhat disconcerted. Then he said:

"You must have come here in a conveyance of some
sort."

"We obtained a hired carriage from the Halt, where
we left our luggage," Atayla said. "The man was willing
to bring us, but I should imagine by this time he has
returned home again."

As if the Earl accepted this as a reasonable state-
ment, he walked away from the door to the fireplace.

He stood with his back to it, looking down at the
sleeping child on the sofa.

The resemblance between them was, Atayla
thought, very obvious, but the Earl's hard face did not
seem to soften.

He merely looked at Felicity as if he hated her and
bitterly resented their intrusion into the Castle.

Slowly Atayla retraced her steps from the door back
to the sofa.

Then as she sat down on the end of it, where she
had been sitting before, Felicity stirred and opened her
eyes.

First she looked round her in surprise, as if she did
not know where she was, then she saw the Earl.

She looked at him for one second before she said a
little questioningly:

"Papa?"

"So you remember me, do you?" the Earl asked
grimly.

"You are Papa!" Felicity said as if she had convinced
herself. "And Mama said you would give me a pony as
you have lots of horses."

"Why should I give you anything?" the Earl asked
sharply, as if he were speaking to a grown-up. "You ran
away and left me."

"I've come back," Felicity replied, "and I'm very tired, and thirsty. I want a drink!"

Atayla looked at the Earl, and after a moment, grudgingly, as if he deeply resented having to give in, he said:

"I suppose you must stay here for tonight. I will tell Dawson to take you to my Housekeeper."

With that he walked from the room before Atayla could reply and shut the door sharply behind him.

Felicity yawned and said again:

"I want a drink. I'm very thirsty!"

"I am sure we will be able to have one in a few minutes," Atayla said comfortingly.

She felt as if she had fought a battle that had exhausted her both physically and mentally, and she knew now how frightened she had been that the Earl might carry out his threat and compel them to leave the Castle.

The Butler came hurrying in to take them upstairs to where an elderly Housekeeper in rustling black, and with a chatelaine at her waist, was waiting for them.

As she climbed the stairs Atayla said a prayer of thankfulness that they had not been turned away penniless and with nowhere to go.

"How can he be so horrible, so offensive, and so aggressive?" she asked herself.

When finally she got into bed, she found herself sympathising with the *Comtesse* for running away, although it was with a man who was already married.

Atayla remembered also the beauty of the white bedroom with its curtains falling from a gold corona, and she had a sneaking feeling that the *Comtesse* had every incentive for leaving both her husband and the Castle.

The bedroom into which they were shown by the Housekeeper, whose name, she learnt, was Mrs. Briercliffe, was certainly awe-inspiring, though at the same time it was comfortable.

The high ceiling, the long windows with curtains surmounted by carved pelmets, and the huge oak four-poster bed, all made Atayla feel that it was part of history, but perhaps not a particularly pleasant part.

"Tomorrow," Mrs. Briercliffe said, "I will open the Nurseries again. But tonight, as you are both tired, I don't expect you want to wait before putting Her Ladyship to bed."

"She is very tired," Atayla agreed. "We have travelled a very long way to come here."

"From Paris?" Mrs. Briercliffe asked, and Atayla knew that was what the Earl had been about to say.

"No, from Tangiers, in Morocco."

"Goodness me!" Mrs. Briercliffe exclaimed. "I never thought of Her Ladyship as being in such a heathen part of the world as that!"

Then, as if she felt embarrassed at having said too much, she busied herself giving orders to the housemaids who were unpacking the trunks which had come with them in the carriage.

Felicity had been appeased by being given milk and biscuits as soon as they got upstairs, but then she complained that her bed was too big.

"I want the room I used to sleep in," she said, as if she suddenly remembered it, "and where's my rocking-horse?"

"It's all upstairs, Your Ladyship," Mrs. Briercliffe replied, "and tomorrow I'll have the rooms dusted and aired for you. They're just as they were when you left them."

"I want my rocking-horse and a pony," Felicity whimpered.

Atayla, who was undressing her with the help of one of the housemaids, answered:

"I am sure you will be able to have those tomorrow, but now you must go to sleep in here, and when you wake up everything will seem different."

As she spoke, she only hoped that she was prophesying accurately.

She had not forgotten what the Earl had said, that they could stay for the night, and she had the uncomfortable feeling that tomorrow he might insist on their leaving.

Only when she had got Felicity into bed did she think of how tired she was herself, and as if Mrs. Briercliffe realised it without being told, she said:

"I'll send something upstairs for you to eat, Miss, and perhaps you will tell Jeannie what you'd like unpacked for you tonight. The rest can wait until tomorrow."

"Thank you, that will be best," Atayla agreed. "Like Her Ladyship, I too am very tired."

"You look done in, and that's a fact!" Mrs. Briercliffe said.

She gave sharp orders to Jeannie to hurry up and unpack the case Atayla indicated, then supervised the tray that was brought upstairs by a footman who arranged it on a table in her bedroom.

Because Atayla felt it would be embarrassing to eat before Jeannie had left, she waited until she was alone, then found that although what was waiting for her in covered dishes looked delicious, she could in fact manage very little of it.

She was so tired that she felt that if she sat down she would never get up again.

She was exhausted not only by the demands of the journey but by the Earl's behaviour and her terror that she and Felicity would be turned away with only enough money to go a few miles, let alone return to Tangiers.

"Why did I not anticipate that this might happen?" she asked herself.

She felt she had been very remiss in not suggesting to the *Comtesse* that the Earl might bitterly resent having his daughter returned to him without explanation or even notice of her arrival.

Finally, when Atayla got into bed, feeling that if she did not do so she would collapse on the floor, she asked herself apprehensively what tomorrow would bring.

She was finding it very difficult to think clearly,

when almost as if he were beside her and speaking to her she heard Father Ignatius say:

"Pray if you need help, and it will come to you."

'I certainly need help now!' Atayla thought a little wryly, and she prayed until she fell asleep.

* * *

Atayla was awakened from a deep slumber by Felicity jumping onto her bed and saying:

"Wake up, Miss Lindsay, I want to go and look at my pony. Mama said Papa would give me a pony, and I looked out the window to see if he was running about on the grass."

With an effort, Atayla brought her mind back from her dream-world to reality.

"If there is a pony," she said, smiling, "I expect he is in the stable."

"Then let us go and find him!" Felicity insisted.

"I think we should have breakfast first."

She sat up in bed and waited for the sleep to clear from her eyes so that she could think clearly.

Then she remembered that Jeannie had said before she left the room the previous evening:

"If you want anything, Miss, ring the bell, and I'll be told you want me, although sometimes it takes a little time as the Castle's so big."

Now Atayla looked round for a bell and found a long embroidered bell-pull hanging beside the bed.

She gave it a tug and wondered how far the wires would have to go from the top before a bell rang which would summon Jeannie to her.

Felicity slipped off the bed to stand at the window where the curtains had not been pulled.

"I cannot see any horses," she said, "but there are little animals that look like goats."

Atayla pulled back the curtains.

"Those are deer!" she said.

"What are they?" Felicity asked.

"They live in the Park," Atayla said, "and they are very beautiful."

"Deer!" Felicity repeated to herself, and Atayla knew she was trying to remember whether she had seen them before.

When Jeannie arrived, apologising for being so long, Atayla asked where they would have breakfast.

"As the Nursery's not yet ready, Miss," Jeannie replied, "Mrs. Briercliffe thought you and Her Ladyship could have it downstairs in the Morning-Room. His Lordship breakfasts in the Dining-Room, but Mrs. Briercliffe thought he would not wish you to join him."

"No, no, of course not," Atayla said.

She thought that nothing would be more embarrassing than to breakfast with the Earl after his behavior of last night.

Because she was also nervous of meeting him, she hurried Felicity down the main staircase.

A footman who was on duty in the Hall escorted them along the passage hung with ancient armour into a comparatively small room, although the ceiling was very high, where breakfast was laid on a table in the centre of the room.

There were several dishes to choose from and a footman to wait on them.

Atayla could not help thinking with a secret smile how very different this was from the discomfort and frugality of the Mission, where she was lucky to have anything to eat and usually was forced to cook it for herself.

Felicity, on the other hand, seemed quite at home, asked for a second helping of a dish she fancied, and finished with toast spread with Jersey butter and honey from the comb.

"I like this honey," she said. "It is nicer than the honey we had in Tangiers."

Atayla was glad she had found something of which to approve, for while she was being dressed she had complained that she had to wear so many clothes, and also that she was cold.

Atayla was hoping that there would be some warm dresses amongst her clothes that were not yet unpacked.

But she had the suspicion that because she had been in a warm climate, her gowns would all be like the one she had first seen her in, of muslin and lace, which would be very unsuitable in the North.

However, she thought, although she was not certain that it was comparatively warm for the time of year, and her travelling-gown with its little jacket seemed quite suitable, although she was hoping that when she finally unpacked she could find another gown to wear.

However, she was far too frightened to allow Jeannie to unpack anything before the Earl had made up his mind to whether they were to stay or leave.

She had known that Mrs. Briercliffe and Jeannie, thinking that the rooms they had slept in last night were to be changed for the Nurseries, had been glad when she said that everything should be left in their trunks until later in the day.

She had not forgotten that there was still some baggage at the Halt, and when she and Felicity came from the Morning-Room, Dawson came towards them down the passage from the Hall to say:

"Your other trunks have arrived, Miss, and I've thanked Roberts for bringing them. He's a difficult man to deal with and sometimes takes half the day to bring us anything left at the station."

"I would like to thank him myself," Atayla said, thinking she should tip him for his kindness of last night.

"He's gone now, Miss," Dawson replied, "but I paid him well for his services."

Atayla could not help a feeling of relief that at least that left her a little more money in her purse, but still, as she was well aware, it was not enough to take her and Felicity many miles from the Castle.

"I want to go and see my pony," Felicity was saying impatiently.

Then with an uncomfortable feeling of constriction Atayla saw the Earl walking towards them.

He was obviously coming from the Dining-Room, and there was a scowl on his forehead, very much as there had been last night.

Atayla held her breath, but Felicity released her hand and ran towards him.

"I want to see my pony, Papa," she said, "and Miss Lindsay says he'll be in the stable. Please, can I go and look at him now, this moment?"

The Earl looked down at her with what Atayla thought was an expression of dislike. Then he said to the Butler:

"Tell one of the footmen to take Her Ladyship to the stables, or better still go yourself. I wish to speak to the lady who brought her here."

He looked at Atayla with what she thought was an expression of even greater dislike.

For a moment she longed to tell the Earl that she had no intention to talking to him and would much prefer to go to the stables with Felicity.

But even as she thought it she knew it was something she could not do, and Dawson put out his hand to the small girl, saying:

"Come along, Your Ladyship, we'll go and look at His Lordship's horses, and very fine they be."

Felicity gave a little skip of excitement. Then when they were moving away Atayla said quickly:

"I think Her Ladyship should wear a coat in case she feels the cold. Perhaps somebody could fetch it for her?"

"I'll see to it, Miss," Dawson replied.

Then he and Felicity disappeared down the passage into the Hall, and Atayla looked up nervously at the Earl.

"Come with me!" he said sharply.

He walked ahead of her as he spoke, and she followed, feeling like a naughty School-girl who was about to be reprimanded for some misdemeanour.

As she walked a few paces behind him, she thought that it was a very Arabian attitude and she was in the place where every woman in North Africa would expect to be.

The Earl opened the door of a room, and as Atayla followed him in, she realised it was the Library and exactly what she thought a Library should look like in any Castle or great house in England.

Her father had often described the joys of being in the Libraries owned by the English nobility, where their collections of books accumulated over the centuries were housed more elaborately than anywhere else in the world.

As she looked at the thousands of books stretching from the floor to the ceiling of the room, which was encircled by a balcony which was reached by a small twisting stairway, she had a sudden longing for her father.

She knew how much he would have appreciated the room and more especially the books in it.

Just for a moment she forgot the Earl and the uncomfortable interview she was about to undergo, simply because she was thinking how fortunate he was to possess something her father had longed for when he was writing his books on the tribes of Africa.

"Goodness knows, it's impossible to do much research on this place," he had said in Algiers, Tunis, Tangiers, or any other place in which they stayed when he was writing down the information he had accumulated while they were travelling.

"Was your Library at home a very large one, Papa?" she had asked.

"It is certainly what I could do with at the moment," her father had replied, "although actually my grandfather and my great-grandfather, who collected most of the books, were more interested in English literature than in anything that came from other countries."

Then he had laughed as he added:

"As you well know, there is very little written work available about my particular subject, otherwise I would not be considered an authority on it!"

"That is true, Papa," Atayla had answered, "and that is why your books are so important."

She was brought sharply back from the past as the Earl said:

"Sit down!"

As he spoke he indicated a chair on the other side of a large Georgian desk at which he sat himself.

It was flanked by high windows embellished at the top with quarterings of the Roth family on the glass.

Through the clear panes the sunshine poured in and brought out the red lights in Atayla's fair hair.

It was a very different colour from the *Comtesse*'s, which was the pale gold of unripened corn.

Without the light Atayla's hair just seemed fair, but when the sun touched it it revealed that there was red amongst the gold, which seemed to glow with a warmth that was otherwise missing.

Her eyes were grey and specked with gold. Because she was thin from her illness, they seemed enormous in her face, and her chin was a very sharp line against her long neck.

The Earl was staring at her and she thought as she had thought last night that there was something insulting in the way he regarded her, but it was difficult to put it into words.

"Now," he said sharply, "I want an explanation from you as to why you are here, and also why you should have assumed that I would accept my daughter, Felicity, after she was taken away from me three years ago."

Atayla's first impulse was to tell him that as she had heard of the *Comtesse* and Felicity only the day before they had left Tangiers, it was impossible for her to answer any questions.

Then it struck her that if she said anything like that, it would give the Earl a good excuse to dispense with her services, and if he kept Felicity and found a Governess for her of his own choosing, she would have nowhere to go.

Because she was very quick-brained, there was only a slight pause before she said:

"I was engaged, My Lord, as Governess to Lady Felicity, and I am here merely because my instructions were to bring her to you."

The Earl looked at her as if he did not believe what she had said. At the same time, it was difficult for him to contradict her.

"What you are saying, Miss Lindsay," he said, "and I think that is the name by which Felicity called you, is that you are here, as one might say, as a paid servant, and it is not your place to question your orders."

He was definitely being rude, and because it made her angry, Atayla looked down at her hands in case he should see by the expression in her eyes what she thought of him.

She told herself that all that mattered for the moment was that she should have a roof over her head and the chance to earn some money before she was dismissed.

"I think, My Lord," she said, "that is an accurate, if unflattering, description of my position."

"If I turn you away, as I intended to do last night, where would you go?"

"Quite frankly, I do not know," Atayla replied. "Although I presume Felicity has other relatives besides yourself, I have no idea where they are or how I could find them."

The Earl's lips tightened and Atayla knew she had been clever enough to put him in a position in which he would find it difficult to carry out his threat of turning her and Felicity out of the Castle.

There was a long pause before he said:

"If I keep Felicity here, are you prepared to stay with her?"

"That is what I hoped I would be asked to do, My Lord. But of course, it is entirely up to you as to how she is taught, and by whom."

As if he found it hard to know what to say, the Earl

rose from the desk and walked across the room to stand with his back to the fireplace, in which a small fire was burning.

"I find this intolerable!" he said after a moment, almost as if he spoke to himself.

Atayla did not reply, as some inner reasoning advised her not to commiserate with him or try to solve his problems.

Then, as he was aware that she was sitting stiffly on the edge of her chair, her back very straight, he said angrily:

"For God's sake, what do you expect me to do? I have heard nothing from anybody about my child, and I had no idea where she was or that she would be arriving until she appeared last night."

"Now she has come home," Atayla said quietly.

"I am only surprised," the Earl said, "that the person who took her from me recognised that as being the truth. At the same time, if I did what I think I have the right to do, I would send the child back to Tangiers, or wherever it is you have come from."

Atayla was just about to say that if he did so, Felicity's mother might be dead when she returned. Then she told herself that would be a dangerous thing to say.

After all, if the *Comtesse* was ill, and Father Ignatius had said she was very ill, there was no reason to believe that she would not recover from whatever it was she was suffering from, and it was certainly unlikely that she would die.

Moreover, if she told the Earl his wife was ill, it might raise his hopes of being free.

'Perhaps there is somebody he would like to marry,' she thought, 'and he would therefore be extremely angry later if it turned out that there was nothing radically wrong with his wife, and I had merely repeated gossip that was not substantiated.'

She therefore said nothing, and after a moment the Earl asked:

"Surely you must have some opinion on this situation as it appears to you?"

"All I am concerned with, My Lord, is Lady Felicity," Atayla replied. "I understand she was not very happy in Tangiers, and that was the real reason for her being sent to Your Lordship."

"What do you mean, she was not happy?" the Earl asked sharply. "If that swine did not treat her properly, I swear I will kill him!"

He spoke so violently that Atayla stiffened and clasped her hands together.

She found the Earl very disturbing. Her heart was beating fiercely and she thought, as she had last night, that his manner was insufferable besides being frightening.

As if he was aware that she was frightened, the Earl said:

"I should not inflict on you my feelings in this matter. At the same time, you do not look at me like an ordinary Governess would. I suppose there was some good reason that you were chosen for the position?"

"I think the only reason was that I also am English."

The Earl stared at her, and she thought this was something that had never crossed his mind.

Although he did say so, she was aware that he was thinking that perhaps it actually had been difficult in Tangiers to find an English Governess, and Felicity's mother, for reasons that were better not mentioned, had not wished her to have one who was French.

"What are you teaching Felicity?" he asked, as if he must assert himself in some way.

"It had not been possible to have ordinary lessons while we have been travelling," Atayla replied, "but I think the first thing she should have now are lessons about England and the English."

She paused, then went on, thinking it out for herself:

"That will be easier, because everything here is new to her, and she cannot remember very much of what she saw and heard when she was only five years old, three years ago."

As Atayla spoke, she thought that the same might almost be said of herself. She too had so much to learn, and she knew already that she was finding it strange, but very lovely, that England was so green and fertile.

After years of moving about the desert, to be able to look all round her and see everything green had a magic all its own.

All the way they had been travelling by train, and even when she was telling Felicity of her strange adventures in Africa, her eyes had been absorbing the landscape, which was so different, and yet, because a child's memory could be very vivid, it was somehow familiar.

"I see your point," the Earl said briefly, "and perhaps when Felicity has settled down we could discuss what subjects would be best for her to study with you, and those for which we must try to find suitable teachers."

Atayla gave an audible gasp, realising as she did so that she had won. They were not to be turned away, and she was to remain as Felicity's Governess.

With an effort she forced herself to reply calmly and quietly:

"I am sure that is the right thing to do, My Lord, and I think for the moment, at any rate, I can cover most subjects which are important for Felicity to study at her age."

As she spoke she rose to her feet, and added:

"Is there anything else Your Lordship wishes to talk to me about?"

"No, Miss Lindsay," the Earl replied. "You have made your position quite clear."

Somewhat belatedly, because she had forgotten it until now, Atayla dropped him a small curtsey.

"Thank you, My Lord."

She walked towards the door and had almost reached it when the Earl said:

"I presume you can ride?"

Atayla almost replied: "Anything on four legs, from a dromedary to a donkey," then decided that would sound frivolous and perhaps impertinent, and instead she answered:

"I have ridden all my life, My Lord."

"Then I will give orders that you can ride with Felicity," the Earl said, "but if my horses are too spirited and too strong for you, do not hesitate to say so."

"I think that is unlikely, My Lord."

She went from the Library, and once she was outside the door she felt like singing and dancing for joy.

She could stay! At least for the moment, she was safe and there was no need to be afraid either of starving or of having to beg the Earl to give her enough money to live until she could find her relatives.

She could not help thinking of how terribly embarrassing that would have been, and how humiliating after the way he had behaved.

"He is horrible and very frightening," she told herself.

At the same time, she had been clever enough to defeat him, and that was all that mattered.

Because she was so excited, she hurried to the stables just as she was, without going upstairs for a hat. Only when she had found Felicity, and saw the Butler's eyes look at her with a slight expression of surprise, did she realise she had been unconventional.

'I must be careful!' she thought. 'Governesses certainly do not walk about outside the Castle without being correctly dressed!'

Then she forgot herself, going from stall to stall, admiring the Earl's superlative horses and feeling wildly excited because she was allowed to ride them.

It suddenly occurred to her that perhaps amongst the clothes the *Comtesse* had given her there was no riding-habit.

For the moment she felt so disappointed that it was

as if her spirits had dropped from the sky down to the earth with a heavy bang.

Then she tried to convince herself that amongst all the things the *Comtesse* had discarded there must be a habit, but she could not entirely banish her apprehension.

Only when they had looked at every horse in the stable and it was growing late in the morning did she take Felicity back into the Castle, where she found that their luggage had been taken upstairs to the Nurseries, which were now ready for them.

The Nurseries were on the third floor, as she had expected them to be. Vaguely at the back of her mind she could remember sleeping and living in a Nursery very like this one when she had stayed with her grandparents during one of her visits to England.

She had also heard her mother describe what her Nursery had looked like as a child.

There was a high guard in front of the fire, a screen which kept out the draught, covered in transfers pasted on it and then varnished, and a big dolls' house, which Felicity ran to with delight and kept saying she remembered.

There were dolls, too—Dutch dolls, patchwork dolls and golliwogs, and a Teddy Bear, a little smaller and older than the one which Felicity had in her trunk.

Now two maids under Mrs. Briercliffe's supervision were unpacking the trunks they had brought with them, and Atayla saw with relief that some of Felicity's dresses were plainer and of warmer materials than the ones she had worn in Tangiers.

However, she must have had them for some time, for they were too short and in some cases needed letting out round the waist.

But Mrs. Briercliffe said this was no problem as a seamstress always worked in the Castle and would soon alter them.

There was fortunately quite a number of coats, and when Atayla told the Housekeeper that she was afraid that the child might feel the chill after living in the heat of Tangiers, Mrs. Briercliffe gave strict instructions that there was always to be plenty of coal in the skuttle and a pile of logs.

Felicity's bed was a very pretty one with frilled muslin curtains decorating a brass bedstead, while in Atayla's room, which was next door, there was an extremely ornate one, again of brass.

"Her Ladyship chose these before His Lordship was born," Mrs. Briercliffe explained. "And that reminds me, Miss Lindsay—Her Ladyship will be expecting to see Lady Felicity before luncheon."

Atayla stared at her in surprise.

"Her Ladyship?" she questioned.

"His Lordship hasn't explained to you that his grandmother, the Dowager Lady Rothwell, is living here?"

"Do you mean she is Lady Felicity's great-grandmother?"

"Yes, Miss Lindsay."

"I had no idea. The child has never mentioned her."

"I expect she has forgotten, Miss," Mrs. Briercliffe said. "Her Ladyship's very old, very old indeed, and you'll find her a little frightening. But, as we often say amongst ourselves, her bark's worse than her bite, although the younger maids are all terrified of her!"

Atayla thought it strange, although she was not quite certain why, that if there was a lady living in the Castle, nobody had ever mentioned it before.

She changed her gown, glad to have something fresh to wear, then a maid came hurrying up to the Nurseries to say that Lady Felicity and Miss Lindsay were to go to Her Ladyship's bedroom immediately.

"You are going to see your great-grandmother, dearest," Atayla said to Felicity. "Do you remember her?"

Felicity put her head to one side as she concentrated on the question.

"Grandmama," she said, as if she was trying to remember. "She made Mama cry."

As this did not sound very encouraging, Atayla said quickly:

"She wants to see you, and mind you are very polite and curtsey to her, and tell her how glad you are to see her again."

"I am not glad if she made Mama cry," Felicity said with unanswerable logic.

"That was a long time ago," Atayla replied. "It is always best to forget the unpleasant things that happened in the past, and think of the nice things that are to happen in the future."

"Like riding one of Papa's horses?" Felicity asked.

"Your father did not say you could ride one of his horses, and you may have to wait until he has a pony for you to ride."

"I shall ride a horse!" Felicity said firmly. "The man showed me one in the stable that he said would be quite all right for me."

"I hope you can do that," Atayla said, thinking that if Felicity could ride, she would be able to do so as well.

The child looked very attractive in a pretty dress that was skilfully smocked on the bodice, and which was worn over frilly lace petticoats, which made it look expensive and elegant, although it was quite plain.

There was a bow of pink satin ribbon in her dark hair, and because she was excited about the horses, her eyes were sparkling and she was smiling happily.

As they walked down the stairs and along the corridor, led by a footman who had waited for them, Felicity holding on to Atayla's hand was giving little skips of excitement.

"This afternoon we will ride for miles and miles," she said, "and very soon I'm going to learn to jump."

She was so thrilled by the idea that Atayla did not like to say that the Earl might not allow her to ride a horse, and she had not yet seen a pony in the stable.

'I shall have to speak to him,' she thought apprehensively. 'I can hardly take the responsibility of her riding anything that is too large for her.'

She was worrying about the horses, and only when the footman stopped outside a high mahogany door at what seemed to be the other side of the Castle did Atayla wonder what the Dowager Lady Rothwell was like.

An elderly maid with white hair and a lined face opened the door, and the footman said, rather unnecessarily as Atayla thought:

"Here's Lady Felicity."

"And about time!" the maid said. "You've not hurried yourself."

"I could only have come quicker if I'd flown," the footman said, "and God didn't give me wings!"

"That's enough from you!" the maid said sharply.

She opened the door wider so that she could look at Felicity.

"My word, Your Ladyship has grown!" she said in a different tone of voice. "Do you remember 'Ja-Ja,' as you used to call me?"

Felicity looked at her, then after a moment she said:

"I can remember my dolls' house."

The maid opened another door and said:

"Here's Her Ladyship, M'Lady, and grown into a big girl since you last saw her."

Because it seemed to be expected of her, Atayla followed Felicity into a bedroom which was very large and very impressive.

At the far end of it was a huge four-poster bed which reached almost to the ceiling, the posts carved to resemble the trunks of pine trees tipped with gold, and on each of the four corners of the canopy was a huge frond of ostrich feathers.

In the very centre of the bed, propped up with dozens of pillows, was the most extraordinary old woman Atayla had ever seen.

Her face was deeply lined, and her eyes were sunk in her head.

She wore what appeared to be a red wig, in which were stuck a number of combs with diamond-encrusted tops, while round her neck were innumerable necklaces of huge pearls, which hung over her shrunken chest onto the sheets in front of her.

Her hands with their swollen fingers and enlarged veins were weighted down with rings which flashed with every movement she made, and her wrists were encircled with diamond bracelets.

She looked so fantastic that Atayla knew that she was gaping at her, and she quickly remembered to curtsey as Felicity advanced towards the bed.

"So, you are back!" the Dowager said to Felicity. "And why have you not come to see us before now?"

"I remember you!" Felicity exclaimed. "I remember all your pretty jewels. You used to let me play with them."

The Dowager seemed pleased, and there was something like a smile on her thin lips as she said:

"That is right! What woman of any age can resist diamonds? Here, put this ring on your finger."

She pulled one from her own hand and put it down on the bed, and Felicity picked it up and put it on her thumb, where it flashed in the light from the window.

"Mama has a bigger diamond than this!" she said.

There was a silence which made Atayla draw in her breath. Then, as if the Dowager knew what she was feeling, she looked at her for the first time.

"You are the Governess, I understand."

"Yes, My Lady, I am Felicity's Governess," Atayla confirmed.

"You do not look like a Governess to me!" the Dowager objected. "Too young, too pretty! What are you after—a husband? You are not likely to find one here."

Atayla stiffened.

She thought she had met some very strange people in her life, but Felicity's great-grandmother was certainly stranger than any of them.

"I am here, My Lady," she said quickly, "to teach Felicity her lessons, especially English."

"I suppose after living in a French household that is definitely a necessity," the Dowager snapped. "I wonder what else besides French she has learnt in the years she has been away?"

The innuendo in the question was unmistakable, and Atayla lifted her chin but did not reply.

Then, as if she wished to find fault, the Dowager said:

"I asked you a question, young woman, or perhaps you think the environment to which my great-granddaughter has been exposed for the last three years is acceptable and something of which you approve."

Atayla thought the question was almost as uncomfortable as those asked by the Earl, and in a deliberately quiet voice she replied:

"I have always understood, My Lady, that one should be loyal to the person by whom one is employed, and that is certainly what I have tried to be."

"I am sure it is an effort," the Dowager remarked. "I am not saying your attitude is not correct, but in my opinion a Governess should look like a Governess!"

"I should have thought it was more important that she should behave like one," Atayla replied, then was sure it was a mistake to have answered back.

Surprisingly, the old woman chuckled.

"So you have a temper, have you? Well, I daresay you are none the worse for that!"

She pulled another ring from her finger and gave it to Felicity. It was a very large emerald, and she said as the child took it:

"Does that please you better? Is it big enough for you?"

"It is very pretty, and very big!" Felicity replied.

"Bigger than your mother's?"

Felicity shook her head.

"Mama does not like emeralds, she thinks they are unlucky."

The Dowager laughed.

"She should know, and I daresay she needs luck."

She put out her hand, which was almost like a claw.

"Give me back my jewels, child. You can play with them another time. Come and see me tonight and bring your Governess with you. I want to keep an eye on her."

"Why should you want to do that?" Felicity asked.

Atayla thought it was a question she would have liked to ask herself.

"People do not deceive me," the Dowager said, and she was not talking to her great-grandchild as she spoke. "I may be old and senile, but I can still see what is in front of my nose."

Felicity did not understand and was bored. She turned from the bed and slipped her hand into Atayla's.

"Come along, Miss Lindsay," she said. "Let us have our luncheon quickly. Then we can go riding."

"Say good-bye to your great-grandmother," Atayla said, "and curtsey as I have told you to do."

Obediently Felicity turned round.

"Good-bye, Grandmama," she said. "I want to play with all your jewels, and have as many rings on my fingers as you have."

"We will see about that," the Dowager answered.

Felicity was not listening.

Once again she had her hand in Atayla's and was pulling her across the room.

"Quickly, quickly!" she said. "I want to ride a big horse and show Papa I am not afraid."

Atayla opened the door and without looking back followed Felicity through it.

Only when they were outside did she think it was without exception the most extraordinary conversation that she had ever had with anybody, and the Earl's grandmother was an exceptionally frightening person.

"What did she mean by saying I do not look like a Governess?" she asked herself.

It could hardly be expected that a Governess should be easily identifiable like a Chinaman or a navvy.

She could understand that she looked too young, and yet a Nursery Governess for somebody of Felicity's age could easily be no more than twenty-one or twenty-two, which Atayla had intended to say was her age if she was asked.

'I may be only eighteen,' she thought, 'but I have done so much and been in so many different places that I am older in my mind if not my body.'

They went up to the Nursery, and Atayla saw that there was a quarter-of-an-hour before luncheon was likely to be served.

"I want you to wait here, Felicity," she said. "I must go downstairs and ask your father if it is all right for you to ride the horse you saw this morning."

"No, do not ask him," Felicity said quickly. "He might say 'no.'"

"He might also say 'yes,'" Atayla replied, "in which case we do not have to worry any more."

"Try to persuade him," Felicity begged.

"I promise I will. So please be good until I come back."

"I will play with my dolls' house."

Atayla, with one quick glance to see that the fireguard was firmly in place, ran down the stairs.

She was nervous of approaching the Earl again. At the same time, she knew she could not take upon herself the responsibility of Felicity riding a horse that might throw her.

'If he refuses,' she thought, 'I can at least press him to get her a pony as quickly as possible.'

She reached the Hall and saw there were two footmen on duty.

"Will you tell me where His Lordship is?" she asked.

"In his Sitting-Room, Miss," one of them replied.

He went ahead of her to open the door, and as she followed him into the room where she had first met him, the Earl looked up from the desk at which he was writing.

Because Atayla was quite certain he would be frowning at seeing her, she felt shy.

She had met so many different people in her journeyings with her father that shyness was something unnatural to her, and she could hardly believe the feeling that made her a little breathless, and it was hard to look at the Earl as she should do.

Then she heard the door shut behind her and knew they were alone, and she walked quickly to the desk.

He made no attempt to rise, and merely waited for her to speak.

For a moment it was impossible to form the words she wanted to say.

Then at last she heard her own voice, rather low and hesitant, begin:

"I apologise for . . . troubling Your Lordship again but Felicity has set her heart on riding one of your horses. Your Head Groom thinks it would be safe enough for her, but I felt I should . . . first ask . . . your . . . permission."

"Why?"

The monosyllable was disconcerting, and because she thought he was being rude it made Atayla's chin go up and it was no longer difficult to speak.

"Because, My Lord, Felicity is your responsibility, and while she has ridden a pony for some time, I need your approval before I take her riding on a horse."

"I should have thought it was something you could have decided for yourself without troubling me," the Earl replied. "Very well, Miss Lindsay, if she wishes to ride one of my horses, I see no reason to forbid her to do so. Remember that most people when they start riding have falls, and the best thing to do is to mount again as quickly as possible."

"I am aware of that, My Lord," Atayla said. "At the same time, Felicity is only eight, and I should have thought that however keen she is to ride and is apparently completely fearless at the moment, it would be better for her to have a pony of the right size."

She spoke firmly, and the Earl's eyes met hers as if he challenged her, and for a moment it was as if there was a silent battle between them.

Then surprisingly he capitulated.

"Very well, Miss Lindsay, I will procure a pony for my daughter. In the meantime, if she rides a horse I am sure Jackson will put her on a very safe one, and either you or a groom can take her on a leading-rein."

"I am very glad to have your permission, My Lord."

She dropped him a small curtsey, then without looking at him again walked from the room.

Only when she shut the door very quietly behind her did she realise that once again she had won a battle.

'This time,' she thought, 'it was against an opponent who was fighting me because he dislikes me personally.'

Chapter Four

Going upstairs from the Morning-Room, where they had had their luncheon because it was thought the Nursery was not quite ready, Felicity was in a wild state of excitement at the thought of riding.

"I am big enough to ride a horse!" she kept saying, and Atayla only hoped that a suitable animal could be found for her.

She had the uncomfortable feeling that if the child had an accident, nobody would care except herself! Then she thought such an idea was a mistake and tried to put it out of her mind.

When they reached the top landing she was surprised to see the Dowager's lady's-maid, whose name she had learnt was Jardine, coming from her bedroom.

When the elderly woman looked embarrassed and hurried past her and down the stairs, Atayla wondered why she should be on the Nursery floor and seemingly so surreptitious about it.

Then she walked into her own room and saw the reason. The maids had unpacked her boxes but had left the wardrobe doors open.

Her gowns were hanging so closely packed together that it was obvious there was not enough room for them, and many were hanging on the sides of the wardrobe.

To Atayla it was unbelievable that all these were hers! Then Jeannie came into the room and said:

"I'm afraid, Miss, we couldn't get all your things in

here, so we've put some of them in the small room next door, which isn't being used."

"Thank you," Atayla answered. "I do seem to have rather a lot."

"I've never seen such lovely gowns, Miss," Jeannie said, "and in such glorious colours!"

Because the maid seemed to expect it, Atayla walked into the next room, which was smaller than her own bedroom, and she imagined that in the past it had been used by a Nursery-maid, or perhaps kept for visiting children.

There was a large wardrobe against one wall and that was also filled with gowns, with some more hanging on the outside of it.

On the bed there was, she saw, a profusion of bonnets and hats of all descriptions, and as she looked at them she wanted to laugh.

Could it be possible that having had not one single garment of her own to wear when she was in Tangiers, she now possessed what any bride would think was a very large and very expensive trousseau?

Even as she thought of it and was very grateful for the *Comtesse*'s generosity, she knew it would be a mistake while she was at the Castle to say who had originally owned the clothes.

"They had better think I was once rich but have come down in the world," she told herself.

That seemed to her quite a reasonable explanation, and she was sure that not only would the servants be shocked at her wearing the clothes that had belonged to the lady who in their opinion had behaved extremely badly, but that the Earl might make it an excuse to dismiss her.

'I must be very, very careful,' Atayla thought.

But when she had the time she wanted to examine every lovely gown and really believe that they would transform her from a very dowdy chrysalis into a brilliant butterfly.

However, there was no time for that at the moment, with Felicity saying:

"Where is my riding-habit? I want my riding-habit."

Atayla and Felicity went to the child's room, which opened out of the Nursery, and Jeannie followed them. As she went, Atayla asked over her shoulder:

"Is there a riding-habit amongst my things?"

"Oh, yes, Miss, and a riding-hat, which I left in the box as I didn't think you'd be wearing it."

"I shall want it," Atayla said firmly, "but first let us dress Her Ladyship."

She found that all Felicity's things also had been unpacked, and the child had several riding-habits.

While some were made of a thin, pretty piqué, which was suitable for Tangiers, others were in a slightly thicker material which had been bought to wear in cooler weather.

She hesitated as she looked at them. Then Jeannie said:

"There's one here, Miss, which seems newer than the rest, and looks like a skirt that's been divided in the middle."

"I can ride side-saddle now," Felicity said scornfully.

However, Atayla realised that if she was to ride a horse it would be far safer for the child to ride astride.

She persuaded Felicity to let Jeannie help her into it, then hurried to her own bedroom to find her own habit.

When she saw it she was very surprised.

She had somehow expected, because the *Comtesse* bought her clothes from Paris, that her riding-habits would be very elaborate and brightly coloured.

She could remember quite well when she was small that her mother's habit, which came from England, had been very plain, and she had said proudly that it had been made by the best habit-maker in the whole of London.

"There is nobody to touch Busvin," her mother had

said, "but, alas, I have never been able to afford to go to him again."

By a strange coincidence, the habit Atayla lifted down from the wardrobe had been made by Busvin and was strictly tailored in a dark cloth that was almost black.

"At least on horseback I shall look conventional, as a Governess should look," Atayla told herself with a smile.

Then she thought it unlikely that the Earl would see her, and his grandmother, who was so critical of her appearance, would be the only person who would be interested in how she appeared.

She dressed herself in the beautifully cut habit, which seemed a little more worn than she had expected.

Then as she looked at herself in the mirror, noting how closely the coat fitted her and how small her waist appeared, she suddenly thought she had been stupid not to think of it before.

Of course the habit had been worn by the *Comtesse* when she was here at the Castle as the Earl's wife.

Atayla immediately felt that it might be recognised by somebody, then told herself such an idea was ridiculous.

One riding-habit looked much like another, and there was no reason for anybody to think that after three years abroad the *Comtesse* would keep anything that was connected with her former life in England.

It took Atayla a little time to tie the white stock round her neck, and she found there were several of them, which Jeannie had put in the drawer with her gloves and handkerchiefs.

She thought perhaps she had made somewhat of a mess of it, but that it did not really matter.

Then, hearing Felicity calling her, she looked round hurriedly for her hat, and as she did so Jeannie came into the room.

"Your riding hat's here, Miss," she said, bringing it to her.

Atayla saw that it was a top-hat which ladies wore out hunting.

She had already arranged her hair very neatly and securely with a number of hair-pins at the back of her head. Now as she put on the hat she thought that even in the hunting-field it would be difficult for any English-woman to criticise her appearance.

At the same time, she could not be certain, and she wished there was somebody she could ask.

"I am waiting, Miss Lindsay," Felicity was saying from the door. "Do hurry!"

"I am hurrying as quickly as I can," Atayla answered, and turned from the mirror.

Jeannie handed her a pair of gloves, and as Atayla saw they were the right sort for riding, she wondered if she would have recognised them herself.

'But at least I have them,' she thought, 'and how very, very grateful I am that I can ride with Felicity and not have to watch her going off with a groom while I am left behind.'

Somebody, she supposed it was Dawson, had ordered the horses to come to the front door, and Felicity was helped into the saddle of a small, lightly built mare which Jackson had chosen for her.

Atayla had a black horse with a white star on his nose that was well trained and quiet.

With a little smile, she thought how amused people would be if they knew the extraordinary animals she had ridden in her years of travelling with her father.

The Arab horses that she preferred were often almost uncontrollable until she could make them realise that she was their master.

However, here she was on a horse, and it was a joy beyond words.

She took the leading-rein which the groom handed her, and as she did so he said:

"Mr. Jackson thinks it'd be a good idea if Oi came with ye, Miss, on your first day."

"I think that is a very good idea," Atayla answered, "and it is very important that Her Ladyship should enjoy her ride and not be afraid."

"I'm not afraid!" Felicity, who was listening, interrupted. "I'm a very, very good rider. *Mon Père* always said so, even though it annoyed him."

They were moving away as the child spoke, and because Atayla was curious she could not help asking:

"Why should it have annoyed him that you rode well?"

"Because I am English and because Mama said once that Papa was the best rider in England."

Atayla did not reply, she merely hoped that the child would not talk of the *Comte* in front of the Earl or the Dowager.

She settled herself comfortably in the saddle and thought that whatever her mount was like, she could not remember when she had ridden in such beautiful surroundings or in such comfort.

The groom, whose name was Jeb, informed Atayla that there was some flat meadowland where it was safe to gallop on the other side of the Park.

They therefore rode carefully through the Park, keeping clear of the low branches of the trees, and Felicity was thrilled at the sight of some small deer which ran away at their approach.

"I want to play with them," she said.

"They are shy and frightened of you at the moment," Atayla replied, "but perhaps when they grow used to you, you may be able to feed them."

"I would like that," Felicity said, "and I would like to have one of my own."

The way she spoke made Atayla realise that like all children she wanted to possess an animal and for it to be hers, and she wondered if it would be possible to ask the Earl if she could have a dog.

Then she thought it was far too soon to start asking for things, and they must, in fact, keep quiet and well out of his way in case he changed his mind and decided not to let them stay.

They reached the meadowland, which as the groom had said was flat and safe for the horses to gallop.

Atayla took Felicity first at a trot before she allowed her to gallop, and realised that the child had not exaggerated when she said she rode well.

'I suppose she really does take after her father,' she thought.

When they reached the end of the meadowland she asked:

"Would you like to try without the leading-rein?"

The child's eyes lit up, and Jeb jumped down to undo the leading-rein and put it in his pocket.

"Do not go too fast to start with," Atayla admonished, "and I will ride beside you."

"Shall we race?" Felicity suggested.

"Not until I am quite certain that you feel safe on your own."

"Of course I do," Felicity said. "I always rode on my own on my pony."

She did not wait to say any more but started off ahead of Atayla, who hastily caught up with her.

They rode to the end of the meadowland, and then as they turned back Atayla saw that Jeb, whom they had left at the other end of the gallop, was not alone.

She wondered at first if the Earl would be angry that Felicity was not on a leading-rein, but thought he could see for himself how well the child could ride, and that it was quite unnecessary for her to be led.

They galloped towards him, and as Felicity drew in her horse she shouted:

"Look, Papa, I can ride a big horse just as well as you!"

The Earl moved nearer to her, and Atayla thought that, however disagreeable he might be, he certainly looked magnificent on the huge black stallion he was riding and seemed very much part of the horse.

"You ride well," he said drily to Felicity, then turned his horse to look at Atayla and say:

"Surely the child is old enough to ride side-saddle? I disapprove of girls trying to pretend they are boys!"

The way he spoke and the note of rudeness in his voice made Atayla reply sharply:

"It is not a question of pretending, My Lord. I merely thought as Felicity was riding a horse for the first time, it was safer for her to ride astride. I also think the pummel on a lady's saddle would be too big for her."

"I have already instructed Jackson to buy a pony for her," the Earl said, "and in future see that she rides side-saddle. I have no use for modern ideas and innovations where women are concerned!"

He did not wait for Atayla to reply, but rode off, and she thought the manner in which he spoke was quite inexcusable.

However, she did not say anything, but when she rode to Felicity's side the child said:

"You are not crying! When Papa spoke to Mama like that, she used to cry!"

Atayla thought, as she had before, that the *Comtesse* doubtless had very good reason for running away from the Earl, but she merely said to Felicity:

"I think we ought to make our way back to the house, and perhaps Jeb will be able to suggest a different route from the one through the Park."

Jeb pointed out a ride through the wood which lay in front of them, which he said would bring them out at the bottom of the garden.

The wood was thick but, Atayla thought, very beautiful.

She began to feel that everything she saw seemed to make her heart respond to it as if it was a part of her childhood dreams, which, even though she had lived abroad for so long, she had never forgotten.

The songs of the birds, the sunshine percolating through the branches of the trees, and when they reached the garden, the flowers, the green lawns, and the trees just coming into blossom were all like a fairy-land after the barren desert, which had seemed to stretch away monotonously into infinity.

"It is so lovely," she said to herself, "and everybody ought to be happy here."

Then she looked at the Castle. It seemed strangely dark and menacing and to be scowling in the same way as its owner did.

As if the thought of the Earl was oppressive and somehow took the gold out of the sunshine, she told herself that all she was concerned with was Felicity, and if she was happy, then she had helped her as the *Comtesse* had asked her to do.

Although Jeb said he would take the horses when they got to the front door, Atayla insisted on riding into the stables, where she told Felicity to thank Jackson for her ride.

"It was Papa who let me ride," Felicity argued.

"But it was Jackson who chose the horse for you, saddled him, and sent Jeb with us to show us the way," Atayla replied, "so you must thank him."

Felicity thought this over. Then she said:

"*Mon Père* did not thank the servants at the Villa. He said they were stupid and inefficient, and sometimes he was angry with them because they did not look after Mama properly."

"Most servants are very glad to be thanked," Atayla said. "If you do not thank people, you may find they do not look after you so willingly."

Felicity obviously thought this over, and when they arrived at the stables she thanked Jackson very prettily.

"Yer gettin' a pony of yer own, M'Lady," Jackson said, "an' Oi knows of one not far from 'ere. Oi'll try to get 'old o' 'im today or termorrow."

"I want a big pony," Felicity said firmly.

"'E be just the right size fer ye as ye are now," Jackson said, "an' a very pretty animal 'e be too."

He turned to Atayla and said:

"'Ow did ye get on, Miss? Oi can see ye're used to ridin'."

"I enjoyed myself very much, thank you," Atayla replied. "But, if it is possible, could I have something a little more spirited tomorrow? I promise you I will be able to manage him."

Jackson laughed.

"Oi can see that, Miss. Oi expects we'll 'ave ye 'untin' before we're finished!"

"I have never hunted," Atayla replied, "but it is something I think I would enjoy."

Then she told herself she was only dreaming. Long before the hunting-season she was quite certain the Earl would somehow have got rid of her.

The idea was depressing, but it persisted in her mind, and when they walked back and up the stairs she thought she must enjoy every moment and miss nothing while she was here.

The Castle might have come straight out of one of her fantasies which were inspired, as she knew, by the stories her mother had told her of life in England.

They went up to the Nursery, where tea was laid out on the round table in the centre of the room.

It was a very English tea, and Atayla could not help comparing the sandwiches, the cakes, the hot scones in a silver dish, and the several jams and honey that were available, with the meals she had had at the Mission.

Then she told herself firmly:

"Forget the past! The future is what should concern you, and making yourself indispensable so that you will not be sent away to starve."

She felt a little tremor of fear at the idea. Then as they finished tea she remembered that the Dowager Countess wanted to see Felicity.

The child had already been changed by Jeannie from her riding-habit into a very pretty and elaborate dress which the maid obviously thought suitable.

Atayla had not interfered, feeling that Jeannie knew better than she did what was expected at the Castle.

However, she found it difficult to select from her huge variety of clothes, which the *Comtesse* had given her, a garment that was plain and in which she hoped she looked correctly attired for a Governess.

The choice, she found, was very limited, for the *Comtesse*'s gowns were all obviously very expensive and, Atayla thought, elaborate, and although she knew she was no judge, they screamed "Paris!" as if it had been written all over them.

However, she found a gown of dark green satin that seemed plainer than the rest and had a bodice of real Venetian lace over which there was a small bolero in the same material as the skirt.

It was exceedingly becoming and made her skin appear dazzlingly white, while it gave a green tinge to her grey eyes.

She only hoped that the Dowager would not notice her, and perhaps she would not be expected to accompany Felicity into her bedroom.

Such an idea, however, was soon dispelled, as Felicity ran into the bedroom crying:

"Can I play with your rings, Grandmama, as you promised?"

The Dowager glanced at Atayla standing in the doorway and said:

"Come here, young woman, I want to see what you are wearing!"

Slowly, because she felt embarrassed, Atayla walked towards the bed.

The Dowager pulled off several of her rings and gave them to Felicity as if to keep the child quiet. Then she exclaimed:

"Very elegant and cost a pretty penny! But who paid for it? That is what I would like to know!"

At the innuendo in her voice Atayla stiffened, and for the moment she could think of no reply. Then the Dowager said:

"You can hardly blame me, living in the wilds of Yorkshire, to be interested and curious as to how a Governess earning a pittance—for who pays them any more?—should be dressed by Worth of Paris!"

Atayla knew then why Jardine had been in her bedroom, and she said coldly:

"It is kind of Your Ladyship to interest herself in me."

"You still have not answered my question."

It struck Atayla that if she said the clothes had been a present from a friend they might guess the friend had been the *Comtesse*, and her instinct warned her once again that it would be very embarrassing to feel that she was, as it were, impersonating the former mistress of the house.

Seeking frantically for some explanation which would conceal the truth, she said:

"I had the necessity of replenishing my wardrobe after being robbed, and fortunately was able to obtain what I required very cheaply."

It sounded to her a somewhat lame explanation, but she could think of nothing else on the spur of the moment.

She knew as she finished speaking that the Dowager did not believe her, but she merely said:

"You certainly 'pay for dressing,' Miss Lindsay, as the saying goes! I can only hope you find an appreciative audience for your appearance."

Atayla thought it wiser not to reply, and after a moment's silence she asked:

"Shall I leave Felicity with you, My Lady, and collect her in perhaps a quarter-of-an-hour?"

The Dowager chuckled.

"That is one way of avoiding answering questions," she said. "Very well, I shall look forward, Miss Lindsay, to seeing your gowns one by one, and I hope you will not disappoint me."

"I hope not, My Lady."

She made a small curtsey and went from the room.

"She is as disagreeable as her son," she told herself, and walked along the passage wondering how she could spend the quarter-of-an-hour until she must return for Felicity.

She thought what she would really love would be to look over the Castle, and she remembered that her mother had said that most ancestral houses had a Curator.

She therefore walked on until she reached the staircase into the Hall and hurried down it to ask Dawson, whom she saw was there:

"Do you have a Curator in the Castle?"

"Indeed we do, Miss. Do you want him?"

"I was hoping he could tell me," Atayla said on the spur of the moment, "where to find some books which would interest Her Ladyship and which could be part of her lessons."

"Will you come with me, Miss?" Dawson asked.

He led the way past the door into the Library to where, on the other side of the passage, Atayla saw as she entered what was an Office. There, an elderly man with white hair was sitting at a desk.

There were a number of bookcases in the room, and also maps of the Estate, which she thought would be interesting to study when she had the time.

"This is Mr. Osborne, Miss," Dawson said, "and you'll find he can tell you everything you wants to know."

Atayla shook hands with Mr. Osborne and explained to him that she wanted some books for Lady Felicity. Then, when Dawson had left them, she asked:

"Please, when you have the time, will you show me the Castle? When I tell you that I have come from abroad and have never seen a large English house or a Castle since I was very small, you can imagine how fascinating it is to me."

Mr. Osborne was delighted.

"I will show you everything, Miss Lindsay," he said, "as soon as you have the time. And, yes, I do have some picture-books which I am sure Her Ladyship would enjoy."

He went into the Library opposite and showed Atayla where on the balcony were some books on travel, many of them illustrated.

Atayla knew Felicity would love to see pictures of Tangiers and other parts of Morocco.

She also found picture-books of English houses, and one where there were illustrations of English birds and, what she was sure Felicity would like, stags of different species.

"These are exactly what I want," she said. "Please, Mr. Osborne, look out for some more which will be suitable for Her Ladyship. You must remember that she has not been in England for so long that there is a great deal for her to learn."

"It's delightful to have her back, Miss Lindsay," Mr. Osborne said. "The place did not seem the same after Her Ladyship left."

Atayla knew he was referring to the *Comtesse,* and she said:

"It must have been very sad for you all."

"Especially for His Lordship," Mr. Osborne said in a low voice. "He's never been the same since he's been alone."

Then he added very quickly in a louder tone:

"I will find you just what you want, Miss, and have them sent up to the School-Room either tonight or tomorrow morning."

The change in the way he spoke made Atayla know instinctively without looking round that the Earl had come into the Library.

She could almost feel his dislike of her vibrating from him when he approached where she was standing with Mr. Osborne.

Then when he reached them she turned her head slowly and saw, as she had expected, that he was scowling.

"I hope you will not damage any books you take from here, Miss Lindsay," he said.

"I promise you that Felicity and I will be very careful with them," Atayla answered. "Apart from these, My Lord, I shall need a number of lesson-books, and of course crayons and pens and other things that are necessary for her lessons."

"You did not think to bring them with you?" he asked.

"No," Atayla replied briefly.

"Was that meanness or spite in the person who paid for them?" the Earl enquired. "Or was it merely your desire to make me responsible for my daughter in more ways than one?"

Once again he was being rude, and Atayla said sharply:

"To tell you the truth, My Lord, I did not think about it."

"Yet you brought a great deal of luggage with you," the Earl persisted, "and not a lesson-book amongst it! How very strange!"

Atayla thought he certainly had a way of finding the weakness in her defence, and for the moment she could not think of a reply.

Then, thinking that attack was the best form of tactics, she said:

"May I, with your permission, My Lord, give somebody a list of what I consider necessary for Felicity's education?"

As she spoke she looked at him defiantly, her chin up, and she thought the scowl between his eyes lightened and he looked almost amused.

"Of course, Miss Lindsay," he replied with exaggerated politeness. "How can I answer that question except in the affirmative?"

"Thank you, My Lord."

Then with an undoubted little flounce of her skirts she walked away from him, carrying the books that Mr. Osborne had given her.

When she went to collect Felicity from the Dowager's bedroom, the child had her hands and wrists covered with jewels, and as Atayla appeared she ran towards her, saying:

"See how beautiful I am! And very, very rich, with so many pretty jewels on my fingers!"

"Where do you think that will get you?" the Dowager asked in her sharp voice.

"I will sell them and buy lots and lots of horses!" Felicity replied.

The Dowager chuckled.

"You could not wear a horse on your fingers or round your wrists."

Felicity laughed.

"That would be funny! But I expect if I am pretty somebody will give me lots of rings and bracelets like these. *Mon Père* gave Mama lots and lots of jewels."

Atayla drew in her breath, and the Dowager said sarcastically:

"Just like her mother! You had better not let my son hear her talk like that."

Atayla was aware that the Dowager was deliberately taunting her with what Felicity had said.

She helped the child remove the jewels before taking her upstairs, and when they reached the Nursery she said quietly:

"Listen to me, Felicity, I want you to promise that you will not talk about the *Comte*, whom you call '*Mon Père*,' any more. Do not mention him to your Grandmama, your Papa, or to anybody else in the Castle. Do you understand?"

"Papa hates him," Felicity said. "I remember he called him a 'dirty Frenchman,' and *Mon Père* said that Papa was a pompous beast of an Englishman!"

"Felicity!" Atayla exclaimed. "You are not to repeat such things or think about them. What happened when you were in Tangiers is not important."

"Papa made Mama cry," Felicity said. "She cried and cried, then we ran away. It was nice in the sunshine, except that *Mon Père* did not like me."

Atayla thought as she had before that Felicity was too intelligent and too quick-brained not to remember what had happened.

To a stupid child it might have meant nothing, but she had the feeling, since in some ways Felicity was like herself, that everything that occurred was stored away in her mind until it was recalled, unfortunately at inconvenient moments.

"Promise me, Felicity," she said aloud, "promise me that you will not mention *Mon Père* to anybody here, and try not to think about him."

Felicity shrugged her shoulders, which was something, Atayla thought, that she must have picked up from the *Comte* or perhaps from some of the French servants he had employed.

"Mama would not let me talk about Papa to *Mon Père*," she said, "and now I cannot talk about *Mon Père* here! It is all very stupid!"

"I agree with you," Atayla said, "but if you want to be happy here, and not make your Papa cross, let us try to do things that will make people happy."

Felicity put her head on one side.

"Can I make people happy?" she asked.

"Of course you can," Atayla answered. "People are unhappy when they do not have love. When you loved your mother you made her happy, and now you must try to love your Papa."

"He does not love me."

"I think he does, inside," Atayla said. "But people are sometimes shy of showing their love for somebody and you have to dig it out of them."

"With a spade?" Felicity enquired.

"Not a real spade," Atayla said, "but you dig out by smiling and saying nice things and paying them compliments, instead of snarling and being disagreeable."

Felicity laughed.

"That is funny!"

"We will make it a game," Atayla said. "You try to make your father laugh and smile, then you will find that he loves you. It is as easy as that!"

As she spoke she thought that it was going to be very difficult for the Earl to accept the child.

At the same time, she suddenly realised that if the Dowager, the Earl, and she went on fighting and scrapping with one another, the person who would suffer most would be Felicity.

'I would take the child away if I had the money to do so,' she thought, 'but this is her home, and I promised her mother I would help her. But it is not helping if she antagonises her father, and if I do the same.'

It suddenly seemed to her that Felicity was very small and vulnerable. She had been taken from one home to another where she was not wanted, and now she had been sent back, like a parcel, without any care, compassion, or understanding.

Atayla knelt down and put her arms round her.

"What is important, darling," she said, "is that you should be happy in this lovely Castle with all those splendid horses to ride. And if you are happy you will make lots of other people happy too."

Felicity looked at her, then quickly, as if it was an impulse that came from her heart, she put her arms round Atayla's neck.

"I love you," she said, "and I like your being with me. Promise you will never . . . never go away and leave me . . . alone."

It was a cry, Atayla knew, of a child who was unsure of herself, and whose sense of security has been disturbed not once but twice.

"I want to stay with you," she replied, "so we will have to try very, very hard to make your Papa like having us here."

Chapter Five

"It's ever so exciting, Miss! What do you think's happening!"

As she spoke, Jeannie seemed to burst into the Nursery, and Atayla, who was reading Felicity a story, looked up in surprise.

"What is it?" she asked.

She did not think that anything which Jeannie called "exciting" was likely to happen, for the last six days at Roth Castle had been very quiet.

Unexpectedly the Earl had gone away, and the house in his absence seemed to settle down into a comatose state.

What was more, the servants seemed more relaxed and certainly much more pleasant to Felicity and to her.

The Chef sent up special little dishes to tempt Felicity's appetite, and Atayla thought that no-one could complain about the excellent suppers she had, with dishes which she had never tasted before but which she knew were French.

She wondered if the Chef had learnt them before the *Comtesse* had run away with the *Comte*.

She could not help being insatiably curious about the past, but she forced herself to ask no questions and to keep reminding Felicity not to talk about the *Comte* and if possible not about her mother.

She thought it was wrong that a child should be restricted in speaking of either of her parents, but at the same time she knew that mention of the *Comtesse* had an explosive quality which she was anxious to avoid.

She had the feeling that the Dowager was watching her, and she still made caustic remarks with innuendoes underlying them which at times were more amusing than unpleasant.

"What do you find to do with yourself, Miss Lindsay," she had asked yesterday, "when there are no gentlemen to admire your smart clothes?"

"Felicity and I have been very busy, My Lady," Atayla replied. "First we explored the Castle, then the gardens, and now we hope to ride all over the Estate."

She thought her soft answer to a rather impertinent question placated the old woman. At the same time, Atayla knew her sharp eyes took in and appraised every gown she wore.

In the same way, as she imagined Jardine had given the Dowager a graphic description of her evening-gowns hanging upstairs, she thought that as she was unlikely to have occasion to wear them, the Dowager would be prevented from making bitter comments and thereby would be disconcerted.

There was no doubt that the Dowager was beginning to grow very fond of Felicity.

The child went eagerly to her bedroom because she could play with her jewels, and to amuse her the Dowager made Jardine fetch and open her huge jewel-case, which Atayla thought was like Pandora's box.

Never had she seen such a profusion of emeralds, rubies, diamonds, and sapphires, besides diamond necklaces, long strings of enormous pearls, and bracelets and tiaras to match them.

To Felicity it was rather like being in an Aladdin's cave. She dressed herself in the necklaces, bracelets, and rings, and finally as a great concession was allowed to put on a tiara.

"Now I look like a Queen!" she said. "Perhaps one day I will sit on a Throne like Queen Victoria."

The Dowager laughed.

"You will have to find a King to marry you first."

Felicity considered this for a moment. Then she said:

"I think really it would be more exciting to live with a Sheikh in the desert, or a Bedouin Chieftain. Miss Lindsay says they have wonderful horses, and their followers either obey their orders or have their heads cut off!"

The Dowager looked at Atayla and said drily:

"A very enlightening history-lesson, Miss Lindsay, but I should have thought it advisable to keep to the more conventional Rulers."

Atayla did not reply that it had not been a history-lesson at which Felicity had learnt this, but part of the story she had told her about her journeys in North Africa.

Felicity was exceedingly curious about them, since while in Tangiers she had seen parts of the rough desert ground outside the city, and it was all very real to her.

However, Atayla thought that to explain this would be a mistake, and she merely said:

"I will certainly take your advice, My Lady."

Then she knew that her meekness made the Dowager look at her in surprise.

Apart from visits to the old lady's bedroom, there was nothing to interrupt the happy hours when she and Felicity rode in the Park, galloped over the meadow-land, and took long rides to explore the Estate.

There were farmers by whom Felicity was greeted enthusiastically, and although Atayla knew that like everybody else they were intensely curious to know why the child had returned, they did not venture to ask any questions.

Because Atayla was having plenty of delicious food, went to bed early, and for the moment was not worried by the thought of being turned away, she slept well and knew that she looked very different from when she had first arrived.

She had put on weight, although she was still very

slim, and her eyes and hair seemed to sparkle with a new brilliance.

The wound on her shoulder had healed, and she no longer had to bandage it, but there was still a tender and very ugly scar.

When she looked at it she hoped fervently that one day, as the Surgeon had promised her, it would fade away into just a thin white line.

She could not help remembering the horror of how it had happened, and how her father had died, but she tried very hard to put such thoughts behind her and, as she had told Felicity to do, to think only of the future.

Already she loved the child, although she had never expected to do so, and she knew that Felicity loved her.

She was aware that she was for the moment the one stable and secure factor in her young life, and only when Atayla was alone at night did she sometimes wonder apprehensively where she could go and what it would mean to Felicity if the Earl should dispense with her services.

Then she told herself that she was being needlessly apprehensive, and that although the Earl disliked her, there was no reason why he should not think of her as a competent Governess for his daughter.

Now at Jeannie's intrusion Atayla looked up with a smile and asked:

"What has happened?"

"You'll never believe it, Miss," Jeannie said, coming farther into the Nursery, "but His Royal Highness the Prince of Wales is coming to dinner tomorrow night."

Atayla stared at her in astonishment.

"Can it be true?"

"Yes, Miss. His Lordship's just arrived back, and he's informed Mr. Dawson that there'll be a dinner-party of fourteen!"

Atayla listened in astonishment, and Jeannie went on:

"His Royal Highness, and of course Mrs. Keppel, are staying with the Marquis and Marchioness of Doncaster, and His Lordship told Mr. Dawson that His Royal Highness has said he wishes to see the Castle, as he's heard a great deal about it. So it's not to be a big party, and Mr. Osborne's to conduct them over the Castle after dinner!"

"Is the King coming here?" Felicity intervened.

"No, not a King, dearest," Atayla replied, "but the Prince of Wales, who will be King one day."

As she spoke, she thought that he had already waited a long time for that position, and Queen Victoria, who had recently celebrated her Diamond Jubilee, looked as if she would go on reigning for many years yet.

But Jeannie had not finished with her information.

"There will be three people staying in the house, Miss: the Marquis and Marchioness of Wick—she's ever so lovely, and she's been here before!—and another gentleman."

Atayla thought the whole thing was certainly surprising, and she had somehow got the impression since she had arrived that the Earl never entertained and was in some ways almost a hermit.

"You'll be able to have a peep at His Royal Highness, Miss," Jeannie went on, "if you come on to the landing when they're arriving. And we've all heard that Mrs. Keppel's very attractive."

Atayla thought she might be going to say something indiscreet about the Prince of Wales's favourite, and gave her a warning glance, but Jeannie was too excited to notice.

"I don't say that I wouldn't have rather seen Princess Alexandra," she said, "seeing how beautiful they say she is. But Mrs. Keppel's the next best thing. That's what the Prince thinks, anyhow!"

She laughed, and Atayla was well aware that the Prince's love-affairs were openly discussed in the Servants' Hall.

She was soon to learn what the Dowager thought about it when she took Felicity to see her great-grandmother after tea.

"I suppose you are all agog like the rest of the household," the Dowager said, "at the thought of seeing a real live Prince!"

"He will be a King one day, Grandmama," Felicity said.

"When he is too old to enjoy it!" the Dowager snapped. "But he has other ways of passing the time, and from what I hear, he is as infatuated with Mrs. Keppel as if he were a young man with his first love-affair."

Atayla thought this was not the sort of thing that should be said in front of Felicity, but fortunately the child was busy bedecking herself with her great-grandmother's jewels.

"Anyway, it will cheer up the gloom of this place," the Dowager said, "and do my grandson good to see a bit of life."

She paused, then as Atayla said nothing, she went on:

"Not that he doesn't do so when he is in London. I have my own way of hearing what he has been up to there."

"I think it is time we went upstairs, My Lady," Atayla said. "Give your Grandmama back her jewels, Felicity, and thank her for letting you play with them."

"Are you pretending to be shocked?" the Dowager asked. "That sanctimonious look in your eye does not deceive me!"

She gave a little chuckle as she said:

"I expect, if the truth were known, you are sorry you cannot go downstairs and show them how alluring you can look in one of your Worth gowns."

"I shall be quite happy to hear about it afterwards," Atayla replied. "I am only sorry for you, My Lady, that you cannot act as hostess for His Lordship."

She spoke very pleasantly, but the Dowager was well aware that she was getting a little of her own back, and she laughed.

"I am too old to care," she said, "but I will wager

you are well aware that you are wasting away in the Nursery, where there is nothing masculine to admire you except a Teddy Bear."

Atayla laughed because she could not help it.

"He is a very attractive one, My Lady!" she replied, and thought as she walked upstairs with Felicity that she had had the last word.

There was no doubt that the idea of the Prince of Wales coming to the Castle galvanised everybody in a way that Atayla found amusing.

When she came down the next morning after breakfast to take Felicity to the stables, so that they could go riding, the whole place seemed filled with people, polishing, brushing, dusting, and cleaning.

'It is like an ants' nest!' she thought, and remembered the huge ones she had seen in the Riff mountains and in other parts of Africa.

There had not been a sign of the Earl since his return, but she could not help feeling an awareness that he was in the house.

It was almost as if, because he was so strong a personality, he vibrated everywhere, and she thought that even if she had not been told he was at home she would have been aware of it.

Jackson greeted them when they reached the stables, and even he, Atayla thought, was thinking of the excitements that were to take place that evening and was not concentrating so much on Felicity's riding as he usually did.

Nevertheless, her new pony, which was a very attractive animal, was brought to the mounting-block and following it was *Rollo*, a horse to which Atayla had taken a great liking.

He was almost completely black except for one fetlock, and was young and inclined to be skittish. She enjoyed the tussles she had with him, knowing that however hard he tried to assert his independence, she could quickly get him under control.

"Oi'm not sendin' a groom wi' ye this morning,

Miss," Jackson said, "an' Oi 'opes ye'll excuse us, but Jeb's got things to do tidyin' up the stables."

Atayla looked surprised because she thought there was no chance of His Royal Highness visiting the stables.

Then she remembered that the Earl had several guests staying in the house, and they would undoubtedly wish to see the horses.

"We shall be all right, Jackson," she replied, and she and Felicity rode off along their usual route across the Park.

"Are we going to have another race this morning?" Felicity asked.

"Yes, of course," Atayla replied, "but this time I will give you a little more of a start than I gave you yesterday."

As she spoke she remembered that she had great difficulty in holding back *Rollo* so as to allow the race to end in a dead heat.

"Today *Dragonfly* and I are going to win!" Felicity said firmly.

They reached the meadowland and were just getting into place when Atayla looked round and saw that they were not alone.

The Earl was coming through the wood on his favourite stallion.

Felicity saw him and gave a little cry.

"Come and join us, Papa!" she called. "I am racing Miss Lindsay, and I will race you too. *Dragonfly* is so fast that I am sure he will beat you!"

The Earl raised his eye-brows, then said to Atayla: "Is this a new idea?"

"Felicity wants to race, and she really rides very well, as might be expected."

For the first time since she had known him, the Earl smiled.

"Is that a compliment?"

"I think actually it is a fact," Atayla replied.

"Very well," the Earl said, "I will race you both."

Atayla looked at the stallion and said:

"Felicity will want a start, and so shall I."

The Earl instantly took over and sent Felicity some way ahead and Atayla halfway between the child and him. Then he counted and gave the command to go, and Felicity set off with a quickness and an expertise which Atayla felt the Earl could not help admiring.

She was so intent on watching Felicity and not letting *Rollo* pass her that they were nearly at the end of the gallop before she realised that the Earl was doing the same thing.

She flashed him a smile to show it was what she had hoped he would do, then as Felicity surged ahead, she deliberately rode a little faster, hoping that she would be able to beat the Earl.

Even as she tried to do so she knew it was hopeless and was aware that it would amuse him to know it.

When they finally drew in their horses, letting Felicity win by half a length, he said:

"One day, Miss Lindsay, I will challenge you without any handicaps."

"Thank you," Atayla replied. "In that case, My Lord, I would like to choose my mount."

"Are you really telling me that you could handle *Green Dragon?*" the Earl enquired.

Atayla knew he was referring to the stallion he was riding, and she said:

"I am quite certain I could."

She saw that the Earl did not believe her, and added:

"I have had the opportunity, My Lord, although you may not believe it, of riding Arabian mares, which I expect you know are always the best and fastest of the herd before they are broken in."

The Earl looked at her in astonishment. Then, before he could ask any questions, she had joined Felicity and they turned for home.

The Earl did not go with them, and as he rode off, Atayla wondered if he had been intrigued by what she had said, or if he merely thought she was showing off to impress him.

"It was nice of Papa to race with us, wasn't it?" Felicity remarked as they rode through the Park.

"Very nice," Atayla replied, "and you must ask him to race you again. If you see him this afternoon, say how pleased you are that he has come home."

"He has not come home to see me," Felicity replied, "but only because he is giving a party for the Prince of Wales."

The way she spoke made Atayla realise that the child wanted the attention of her father, and because Atayla had loved her own father so much, she knew how much the Earl could mean in his daughter's life if only he could forget how her mother had taken her away for three years.

It was a cruel thing to do, and yet in some ways Atayla could not help feeling, because she was so beautiful, so fragile, and obviously very sensitive, that in the Castle the *Comtesse* must have been like a song-bird imprisoned in an iron cage.

Even if she had loved the Earl and he had loved her, it could have been a difficult and frustrating life for a very young girl.

Atayla wished she knew more of the truth about their marriage, but she was too proud to ask questions of the servants even if they had wished to talk.

However, she was certain that as the Dowager obviously hated the Earl's wife, anything she could learn from her would be prejudiced.

"It is rather like reading a story in a book and coming in halfway to find all the characters reacting very strangely to what has happened," she told herself, "but the first chapters have somehow been lost."

She smiled at her own fantasy, then wondered whether Felicity missed her mother, and if the child ever lay at night, as she did, longing for her father with such intensity that it was a physical pain.

* * *

Everything at the Castle seemed as if a whirlwind was sweeping through it, and everybody was running about rather than walking.

Later in the afternoon, Atayla was aware that the Marquis and Marchioness of Wick had arrived, and when Jeannie came upstairs after tea, she apologised for not having helped Felicity as she usually did out of her outdoor clothes.

"They're a bit short-handed downstairs, Miss," she said to Atayla, "because Miss Jones has one of her headaches."

Jones was the elderly housemaid who worked under Mrs. Briercliffe, and her headaches were frequent and so intense that she had to lie down.

"It means I've got a lot more to do," Jeannie said, "and although Her Ladyship's brought her own maid with her, she's feeling poorly after being in the train, and we've all got to give a helping hand."

"Do not worry about us," Atayla said. "I know you want everything to go smoothly and be at its best for His Royal Highness."

"We do indeed!" Jeannie said. "And don't forget, Miss, I'll come and fetch you to see the Marchioness going down for dinner, and the Royal Party coming in through the front door."

"It all sounds very exciting," Atayla said.

She was aware, because her father had told her, that Royalty were always greeted by the host himself on the doorstep, and seen off in the same way.

"In England it is only Royalty who receive such attention," he said, "but in Arab countries, as you know, my dear, every host whether in a tent or a house meets his guests and speeds their departure with exquisite good manners."

Atayla knew this was true and was interested by the courtesy which Arab Chiefs always showed their guests.

She was aware that one had only to praise a possession of one's host, whether it was an *objet d'art* or a beautiful woman, for its owner to reply:

"It is yours!"

"Does one really take it away when leaving?" Atayla had asked.

Her father laughed.

"If that happened, I should have a numerous Harem by now! No, you accept the gift with gratitude, then conveniently forget it has been given to you."

'I shall watch the Earl receiving His Royal Highness,' Atayla thought, 'and see if he is as hospitable as a Bedouin Chieftain, or the Sheikh who entertained Papa and me with a huge feast at which we were expected to eat the special delicacy consisting of the eyes of the sheep which had been roasted for us.'

Then she told herself her mother would have been shocked at her peeping and peering, thinking it beneath her dignity.

"If I were a Lady, that would be true, Mama," she said, as if her mother was listening, "but I am merely a Governess and, as the Earl pointed out to me, a paid servant."

She put Felicity to bed, heard her prayers, and kissed her good-night.

"Do you think Papa will race with us tomorrow?" Felicity asked.

"He will probably have to look after his guests," Atayla replied, "but I am sure when they have gone he will be willing to race again, if you ask him nicely."

"I will do that," Felicity said, "but I think Papa would be very surprised if I kissed him as I kiss you."

"Try it and see," Atayla advised. "Perhaps he wants you to kiss him, but feels that he does not like to ask you, in case you don't want to."

Felicity thought this over for a moment, then she said:

"I would like to kiss Papa. The servants all think him very handsome, and so do I."

"Then you kiss him," Atayla advised.

She turned out the light and knew when she left Felicity's bedroom that she was almost asleep.

She undressed and had her bath as she did every night before dinner, and was just thinking of putting on one of the comfortable, loose tea-gowns which were amongst the clothes the *Comtesse* had given her, when there was a knock on her bedroom door.

When she called out: "Come in!" she saw to her surprise that it was Mrs. Briercliffe.

She had not expected that the Housekeeper when she was so busy would climb the stairs to the Third Floor.

"I've come to tell you, Miss," Mrs. Briercliffe began rather breathlessly, "that His Lordship's instructions are that you're to dine downstairs tonight."

"Dine downstairs?" Atayla repeated in astonishment.

"You'll have to hurry, Miss, because His Royal Highness'll be arriving in under an hour."

"I do not know what you are saying!" Atayla said.

"It's Lady Bellew, Miss, who was to be one of the dinner-party. She lives only about two miles from here, and her husband's the High Sheriff."

Atayla looked bewildered as Mrs. Briercliffe went on:

"A groom has just come with a message to say that Her Ladyship's very sorry, but she's stricken down with such a bad cold that she's unable to dine tonight."

"Is her husband coming?"

"Yes, Miss," Mrs. Briercliffe replied, "but that makes the dinner-party thirteen, and it's quite impossible to get anybody else at such short notice."

Atayla gave a little laugh.

"Are you saying, Mrs. Briercliffe, that His Lordship has really asked me to dine with his guests?"

"Yes, Miss, and very pretty you'll look in one of them lovely gowns of yours, which I thought you would never have the chance of wearing."

"That is what I thought too," Atayla agreed.

It seemed so incredible that she should dine with the Prince of Wales and the Earl's other guests that she felt she must be dreaming or had not heard correctly what Mrs. Briercliffe had told her.

Then, because it was an excitement she had certainly never expected to happen, she jumped to her feet and said:

"The difficulty, Mrs. Briercliffe, will be to decide which gown I should wear! Can Jeannie come and help me? I am sure you are too busy."

"I am indeed, Miss, but when His Lordship told me to tell you to come downstairs, I thought it only right that I should come myself, to inform you that you were invited."

"And I am thrilled to hear it!" Atayla replied. "It is so utterly unexpected."

Mrs. Briercliffe smiled at her enthusiasm, then said:

"There will not be a lady at the table, Miss, as'll look prettier and smarter than you, and that's a fact!"

"Thank you."

Mrs. Briercliffe went towards the door.

"I'll send Jeannie to you, Miss, and don't you be late! The guests all have to be downstairs in the Drawing-Room before His Royal Highness arrives."

"I will not be late," Atayla promised, and started to brush her hair.

As she did so she was thinking how glad she was that she had washed it only the night before, and it was now soft, silky, and shining.

However, she thought it would be a mistake to try any new arrangement that she had not practised before, and therefore she swept it from her forehead and coiled it at the back of her head in a chignon.

She was just putting in the last hair-pins when Jeannie came hurrying into the room.

"Oh, Miss, I couldn't believe it when Mrs. Briercliffe told me you'll not only see the Prince but speak to him! It's ever so thrilling, it is really!"

"I have to choose the right gown to wear, Jeannie," Atayla said. "Which one do you think would be the most becoming?"

Jeannie thought for a moment. Then she said:

"I knows the one I'd like to see you in, Miss. I thought when I unpacked it that it was just like a bit of sunshine, and that's what's often wanted in this place!"

Because she had thought she would never wear them, Atayla had moved all the evening-gowns out of the wardrobe in her bedroom and into the smaller room next door.

Jeannie now disappeared into the next room and came back holding high in the air so that it did not touch the floor a gown that Atayla had, in fact, thought was one of the prettiest that the *Comtesse* had given her.

Of very pale gold, which actually was the colour of her hair, it was heavily embroidered round the hem, which was held out by frill upon frill of gauze, all of which sparkled with gold sequins.

The sequins made a pattern on the skirt and decorated the bodice, and the frills which encircled the décolletage formed small, puffed sleeves that covered her upper arms.

What was fortunate, Atayla thought, was that the gown was cut in such a way that it would hide completely the scar on her shoulder.

When Jeannie had buttoned her into it she saw she had been right in anticipating this, and also that the dress accentuated the tininess of her waist and gave her a grace she thought she had never had before.

It was certainly like a ray of sunshine, and because it was so skilfully embroidered, she felt she would not feel a lack of the profusion of jewels which every other lady in the party would be wearing in the Royal presence.

Somebody had told her, although Atayla could not remember who it was, that the Prince of Wales expected any woman with whom he dined to wear a tiara.

"Tonight he will be disappointed!" she told herself.

Then Jeannie exclaimed:

"Did you know, Miss, there's some little bunches of

flowers made from the same material as this gown and embroidered with the same sequins?"

"No, I did not know," Atayla answered. "Where have you put them?"

Jeannie ran into the next room and came back with two tiny bunches which glittered and shone almost as if they were jewels.

She fixed them on each side of the chignon, and Atayla felt they gave a finish to her appearance that she had not had before.

There were long gloves to be worn that were of such a fine, delicate suede that they were unlike any gloves Atayla had ever seen.

Like the *Comtesse*'s shoes, they were a little tight, but she knew it would be *lèse-majesté* to shake hands with the Prince of Wales unless she was wearing gloves.

"You looks lovely, Miss, you really do!" Jeannie said when she was dressed. "If Mrs. Keppel's jealous of you, I'll not be a bit surprised!"

Atayla laughed.

"I think that is very unlikely."

At the same time, as she went down the Grand Staircase she was aware that her heart was beating tumultuously, and she felt excited in a way she had never felt before.

She was to see for the first time the way of life that her mother had described to her as being hers before she had married her father.

Atayla had known, because there had often been a wistful note in her mother's voice when she spoke of the Balls she had attended and the parties her father and mother had given for her, that she longed for her own daughter to be part, as she had been, of the Social World.

"I am afraid, dearest," she had said to Atayla, "that it is something that will never happen, but I would love to have presented you at Court and watched you waltz at your first Ball with a lot of handsome young men."

"I may not be doing that tonight, Mama," Atayla

said to her mother in her heart, "but I shall be meeting
the Prince of Wales, and you must help me not to make
mistakes which would make you ashamed of me."

Dawson was waiting at the bottom of the staircase,
and she knew as she saw the expression on his face that
he was very surprised at the way she looked, and at the
same time delighted.

"You're a sight for sore eyes, Miss!" he said, and the
way he spoke made Atayla laugh.

He went ahead of her across the Hall and opened
the door into the Drawing-Room.

It was a very impressive room, which Atayla had
briefly explored with Felicity, but now that the huge
chandeliers were lit, it had a beauty she had not
expected.

The austerity of it had been swept away because
there was a profusion of flowers everywhere, and Atayla
felt as if she were walking onto a stage!

The difficulty was that she was not certain what her
role entailed.

There were two men at the far end of the room, and
Dawson announced:

"Miss Lindsay, M'Lord!"

For a moment she felt so shy that everything
seemed to swim in front of Atayla's eyes.

Then she realised that the Earl was walking towards
her, and because it was the first time she had seen him in
evening-clothes, she thought he looked not only most
impressive wearing several decorations on his chest but
even more awe-inspiring than usual.

As he reached her he said:

"I am very grateful to you, Miss Lindsay, for
helping me out of what would otherwise have been a
disastrous situation."

He must have been aware that she thought his
description was somewhat exaggerated, for he explained:

"His Royal Highness has a horror of sitting down
thirteen. In fact, he refuses to do so, and I should have

found it very difficult to know who should be sent away from the door."

"I am very grateful to be allowed to be of use, My Lord," Atayla replied.

As they were talking they had walked towards the hearth-rug, and the Earl said:

"May I introduce Sir Christopher Hogarth, an old friend of mine? Christopher, this is Miss Lindsay, who has so obligingly saved the situation at only a few minutes' notice."

Sir Christopher, who was a good-looking man and, Atayla thought, a little older than the Earl, said:

"I can only imagine, Miss Lindsay, that you obliged our host by dropping down from a star in the sky, or perhaps you were the last ray of sun left behind at sunset!"

Atayla laughed, and the Earl said:

"You are very poetical, Christopher!"

He did not make it sound exactly a compliment, but before Sir Christopher could reply, the Butler announced:

"The Marquis and Marchioness of Wick, M'Lord!"

The Marquis was an elderly man, and the Marchioness was middle-aged but very attractive.

She was glittering with jewels and wore a diamond tiara, but Atayla thought that while her gown was extremely elaborate, it was not as sensational as her own.

They were introduced, then the Earl glanced at the clock and said:

"I had better take up my position in the Hall. I am sure Doncaster, who is extremely punctilious on the race-course, will get His Royal Highness here exactly on time."

"I will act as host until you return, Valor," Sir Christopher said, "and I cannot imagine a more pleasant task."

It was obvious that he knew the Marchioness well, and she talked to him animatedly, but Atayla was aware that even while he listened his eyes were on her.

It made her feel less shy and more sure of herself to know that at least one person in the party admired her, and she said a little prayer of thankfulness that the *Comtesse* had included evening-gowns amongst the other things she had given her.

She could not imagine anything more frustrating than if after the invitation to join the party she had had to reply that she could not accept as she had nothing to wear.

'That is something I will not be able to say for years and years,' she thought.

She felt as her gold sequins sparkled in the light of the candles that it was all like a dream, and she only hoped she would not wake up too soon.

* * *

The Prince of Wales was very stout, very genial, and obviously in a good temper.

A member of the party was the Portuguese Ambassador, the Marquis of Soveral, who, although Atayla was not aware of it, could always manage, because he was a great wit, to keep the Prince in a good mood, and was therefore included in almost every house-party to which His Royal Highness was invited.

Mrs. Keppel was a little stouter and a little older than Atayla had expected, but there was no doubt that, if not strictly beautiful, she had a fascinating face, and the Prince's eyes when he looked at her were very revealing.

There was champagne to drink before dinner, and Atayla thought it seemed to make everything that was said by the guests sparkle like the bubbles in the glasses, and when she was taken in to dinner on the arm of Sir Christopher, she said:

"This is very, very exciting for me!"

"Our host tells me you are Governess to his daughter, Felicity. Can that be true?"

"I do not know why you sound so surprised," Atayla answered. "I am actually a very proficient Governess!"

"I can picture you doing a great many other things rather better," Sir Christopher said. "And why have you

chosen to bury yourself in a Castle that should exist only
in one of Grimm's Fairy Tales?"

Atayla laughed.

"I like being here," she said, "and I am only afraid
that I will not be allowed to stay and will have to go
elsewhere."

"Why should anybody want to turn you away," Sir
Christopher enquired, "least of all your host?"

Atayla did not answer, and he said:

"As an old friend of Valor's, I gather it was a
tremendous surprise when his daughter was returned to
him after being kidnapped in that appalling manner
three years ago."

"Kidnapped?"

"There is no other word for it," Sir Christopher said.
"Nadine left and took the child with her without explanation or warning."

Atayla thought it best to say nothing, and after a
moment Sir Christopher said:

"To look at, Nadine was one of the most beautiful
women I have ever seen. Is she still as lovely?"

Again Atayla hesitated, and he said:

"There is no need to pretend to me, Miss Lindsay.
Valor told me that you arrived completely unexpectedly
and uninvited from Tangiers, and as the only person who
would have sent the child back to her father was Nadine,
presumably she engaged you as a very unlikely-looking
Governess."

Atayla laughed.

"What exactly should a Governess look like?" she
asked. "People always seem to be complaining about my
appearance!"

"Are you surprised?" Sir Christopher enquired.
"And dressed as you are now, no-one would suspect for
one moment that you were anything but a Professional
Beauty, and in exactly the right place, being at a party
given for His Royal Highness."

Atayla had heard about the Professional Beauties
whose post-cards sold in their thousands, and who, even

though they were Society Ladies, were acclaimed as if they were actresses.

She supposed it was a compliment to be told that she was one, but at the same time she was not quite sure.

"Well?" Sir Christopher said. "I am waiting for an answer to my question."

"I think it would be a mistake," Atayla replied in a low voice, "to talk about the past, which would obviously upset the Earl. So it is something on which I prefer to remain silent."

Sir Christopher smiled.

"That is very wise. At the same time, you might tell me what you were doing in Tangiers."

"I had not been there long, having in fact come there from Moulay Idriss."

Atayla was being deliberately provocative, thinking that Sir Christopher would never have heard of the Holy City in the Zerhoun Hills, and she was also trying to divert his mind from the *Comtesse*.

But to her astonishment he looked at her sharply and said:

"Lindsay! You cannot be any relation of Gordon Lindsay?"

"He . . . he was my . . . father!"

"I do not believe it!" Sir Christopher exclaimed. "Then how, of all places, have you landed up here?"

"You knew my father?"

"I have admired him and have read everything he has written. Moreover, although you may find it an amazing coincidence, my mother was a Lindsay!"

Atayla drew in her breath.

"She was . . . one of Papa's . . . relations?"

"A very distant one, but when she was alive she was an extremely well-read and well-educated woman. It was she who first showed me your father's books and the articles he wrote in the *Royal Geographical Magazine*."

"And you enjoyed them?"

"I was enthralled by them!" Sir Christopher replied.

"Papa had finished a book about the Berbers just before he died."

"He is dead?"

"He was murdered by robbers," Atayla replied. "We were on our way home to Tangiers, a very small caravan with few servants with us. The robbers swooped down from the hills and everybody was . . . killed except me."

"How did you survive?"

"They left me for dead, but I was carried by some kind people to Tangiers and nursed in the Mission."

"It is the most fascinating story I have ever heard!" Sir Christopher said.

Atayla looked towards the top of the table to where the Earl sat looking, she thought, almost as if he himself were Royal. Without asking herself why, she said to Sir Christopher:

"Please do not say anything to anybody here . . . will you promise me? . . . as to who I am and where I come from."

"Are you telling me our host does not know that your father was Gordon Lindsay?"

"He just thinks I am a Governess chosen by Felicity's mother," Atayla said, "and that is how I would like to leave it."

She did not know why she wanted to be secretive about it. But perhaps she was afraid that the Earl would think that she was therefore incompetent to teach Felicity in a civilised country, or perhaps he might disapprove of the life she must have led with her father.

"Please," she begged, "promise me you will say nothing."

"Of course," Sir Christopher answered, "but only on condition that you tell me what latest discoveries your father made and all about his new book, which I shall order immediately from the publishers."

"It is very, very interesting," Atayla said.

They went on talking, and it was only when dinner had been in progress for quite a long time that Atayla remembered she should turn and talk to the gentleman on her other side.

With an effort, because she had found it fascinating to find anybody who was so interested in her father and knew so much about him, she turned to her left.

But she discovered that her other dinner-partner, an elderly Peer, was deep in conversation with the lady beside him, discussing the horses that were running in the Spring meeting at Doncaster.

As they obviously had no wish to be interrupted, she turned back to Sir Christopher, and he said with a smile:

"Fate has played into our hands, since the lady on my other side seems equally engrossed! So now we can continue what to me is one of the most exciting conversations I have had for a long time!"

They talked about her father's other books, of his latest discoveries regarding the Berbers, and of what he thought of the way the French had established themselves in Algeria after the Battle of Isly.

It was so long since she had talked of such things to anyone to whom they meant anything that Atayla's eyes were shining like stars.

More than one of the Earl's guests asked who she was with an inescapable expression of admiration in their eyes.

Only when the ladies retired to the Drawing-Room was Atayla aware that one or two of them were regarding her with somewhat hostile looks, until Mrs. Keppel asked her to sit down beside her.

"I hear you are looking after our host's daughter," she said. "Does she look like her mother? I remember seeing her some years ago and thought her very beautiful."

"Felicity more resembles her father."

"Nobody could be more handsome," Mrs. Keppel remarked, "but it is a pity the child is not a son."

"Why?" Atayla enquired.

"Because as things are," Mrs. Keppel replied,

"there is no chance of his ever marrying again, although naturally, like every man, he wants an heir."

"Yes, of course," Atayla agreed. "I had not thought of that."

"But what could be a more delightful place in which to bring up children?" Mrs. Keppel said. "I am so looking forward to exploring the Castle after dinner, and His Royal Highness is particularly interested in seeing the Library."

As soon as the gentlemen joined the ladies, the Earl said that those who wished to see the Castle could come with him and meet Mr. Osborne, who was waiting in the Hall.

But, he added, anybody who preferred it could stay in the Drawing-Room, where card-tables had been erected for those who wanted to play games.

"Personally," Sir Christopher said, "I want to talk to you, Miss Lindsay."

"I am not quite certain," Atayla replied, "whether I am expected to stay or go."

"What do you mean by that?"

"I was only asked down to make up the fourteen at dinner, and no-one has told me what I should do now when there is no more necessity for my presence."

"There is every necessity as far as I am concerned," Sir Christopher said, "and I have no intention of letting you leave. So let us sit on the sofa while you go on telling me about your father's discoveries."

"Have you ever been to Africa?"

"Several times," he answered, "for big-game hunting and shooting, but not in the parts where you have been. Now tell me what your father thought about the Riff mountains."

There was so much to say that when the Royal Party returned from touring the Castle, Atayla thought they could only have been away for about five minutes.

However, the Marquis of Doncaster said:

"I think we should be leaving now, Valor. His Royal Highness is going back to London tomorrow, and we, as you know, will have to be at the race-course early in the morning."

They all shook hands, and as Atayla made a deep curtsey to the Prince, he said:

"You are very pretty, my dear, and if you ever come to London you will be a sensation! I shall certainly welcome you at Marlborough House."

"Thank you, Sir."

However, she felt as he turned away that that was something which would never happen. At the same time, she knew her mother would have been pleased at what the Prince had said.

Then as the Earl escorted the Royal Party to the front door, she thought it would be sensible for her to leave too.

"I am going to bed now," she said to Sir Christopher. "Please, keep your promise."

"I never break a promise," he answered, "and I shall look forward to seeing you tomorrow, when you can tell me more about your father. Besides, do you realise that, if somewhat distantly, we are related?"

"That means a great deal to me, because I have no idea where in England I have any relations," Atayla said.

Because she felt he would want to talk to her about it, she quickly said good-night to the Marquis and Marchioness of Wick, and hurried from the room before Sir Christopher could prevent her from doing so.

She did not go up the main staircase, where the Earl might have seen her. Instead, she slipped away down the passage which led to a secondary staircase, and there she climbed up to her own bedroom.

When she reached it, she thought it was the most exciting evening she had ever spent, and because she could not help expressing it in some way, she twirled round and round in the Nursery, swinging her skirts round her ankles.

"It was lovely, lovely, lovely!" she said aloud. "Thank You, God, for letting it happen!"

Chapter Six

Atayla was fast asleep when she was awakened by the sound of the door opening, and she thought to her surprise that it must be time for her to be called.

Then she heard Jeannie's voice saying:

"Sorry to disturb you, Miss!"

She opened her eyes to see Jeannie standing just inside the door with a candle in her hand, fully dressed but rather untidily, with her white cap crooked on her head.

"What is the matter?" she asked.

"I came to ask, Miss, if I could borrow your bandages," Jeannie replied.

It struck Atayla that something might have happened to Felicity, and she sat up quickly.

"What is it? Who has been hurt?"

"It's the Marchioness, Miss. She's cut her hand, and as I knew you had some bandages, I thought it'd be quicker to come to you than to wake Mrs. Briercliffe."

"Yes, of course," Atayla said.

"Can I get them, Miss? I think they're in a drawer over there."

Jeannie walked across the room, and Atayla asked:

"How did the Marchioness cut herself?"

"With a glass, Miss, an' her hand's bleeding badly."

"You will have to wash it before you bandage . . ." Atayla began, then stopped. "I had better come and do it."

She remembered how many people she had band-aged when she was travelling with her father, and she knew she would be far more skilful than Jeannie.

The maid gave a sigh of relief and said:

"I'd be ever so grateful, Miss, but I don't like to trouble you."

"It is no trouble," Atayla replied.

She got out of bed and put on over the diaphanous nightgown which the *Comtesse* had given her a loose negligé of chiffon and lace.

She thought when she wore it that she would have to get something thicker before the winter, but that did not concern her now, and without bothering to look in the mirror she followed Jeannie to the door.

"The quickest way," the maid said, "is along the top of the house and down another staircase."

"I will follow you," Atayla replied, and without saying any more Jeannie set off quickly, the candle flickering in her hand.

Atayla realised that they were walking along the top floor of the Castle, where she thought the maid-servants slept. Then, after going a long way, they descended a narrow staircase which on the next floor gave way to a wider one, which was thickly carpeted.

When they reached the end of that staircase, Atayla realised they were in the corridor which led to the bedrooms where she and Felicity had slept their first night at the Castle.

She had the idea that at the end of it, not far from the staircase by which they had descended, there was the Master Suite of rooms where the Earl slept.

However, she had little time to think of anything but keeping up with Jeannie, and now it was easier to see where they were, as there were a few gas-lights left burning in the corridor.

Jeannie walked on, knocked at a door and then opened it, and Atayla realised that the Marchioness was sleeping in the room which Felicity had occupied and which contained a large four-poster bed.

She was alone, and Atayla suspected that the Marquis was sleeping in the next room, which she had occupied.

The Marchioness was sitting up in bed with a hand-towel wrapped round her hand, and it was already deeply stained with blood.

"I've brought Miss Lindsay, M'Lady," Jeannie said. "I'm sure she'll bandage you better than I can."

"It is very kind of you, Miss Lindsay," the Marchioness said gratefully. "I understand my lady's-maid took a sleeping-potion before she retired to bed, and it is impossible to wake her."

"I am very experienced at bandaging," Atayla said. "How did you hurt your hand?"

The Marchioness explained that reaching out in the darkness for the glass of water which stood beside her bed, she had knocked it against a heavy candlestick and the glass had broken in her hand.

She undid the linen hand-towel as she spoke, and Atayla saw that she had cut several of her fingers on the inside, and also the base of the thumb.

She was sure they were only surface wounds, but, at the same time, they were bleeding profusely.

She sent Jeannie to fetch a basin of water, and washed the Marchioness's hand very carefully before she put a pad of lint and cotton-wool on it to stop any further bleeding.

Then she bandaged it with a skill which could only have come from having done the same thing many times in the past.

"You have done that beautifully, Miss Lindsay!" the Marchioness exclaimed when she had finished. "Just as good as any Nurse!"

"I am afraid it will hurt you a little," Atayla said, "but try not to move it too much and start it bleeding again. You had better see a Doctor in the morning."

The Marchioness sighed.

"How could I have been so careless?" she asked.

"But that is what everybody asks after an accident has happened."

Jeannie emptied the water into a china pail beneath the wash-hand-stand and picked up the pieces of broken glass very carefully. Then she collected the bandages and was obviously anxious to return to her bed.

"Try to sleep," Atayla said to the Marchioness, "or perhaps you would like a drink first, as you were prevented from having one."

"I am rather thirsty," the Marchioness admitted.

Atayla looked at Jeannie.

"Go back to bed," she said. "I know you have to get up early."

"Thank you, Miss," Jeannie answered. "I'll leave the candle at the bottom of the stairs."

She slipped away, obviously glad to be released, and Atayla walked to the wash-hand-stand, found another glass, and filled it with water from a glass bottle.

She took it to the Marchioness, who drank it thirstily.

"I suppose," Atayla said, "I ought really to get you a cup of tea or something warm to drink, after what has been a shock, but I am afraid I should never find my way about the Castle as I would in an ordinary house."

The Marchioness gave a little laugh.

"No, indeed," she agreed, "but I am quite all right now. Just angry at my own stupidity."

"You will feel better in the morning," Atayla said consolingly.

She took the empty glass from the Marchioness and put it back on the wash-hand-stand in case she should knock it over again. Then she blew out the candle by the bedside, and by the light from the passage outside found her way to the open door.

"Good-night, My Lady."

"Good-night, Miss Lindsay, and thank you for being so very kind," the Marchioness replied.

Atayla realised that all the time she was in her room, the Marchioness had spoken in a low voice, and

she was certain she was doing so because she did not
wish to disturb her husband in the next room.

She started to walk along the passage the way she
had come with Jeannie, thinking as she did so of some of
the accidents that had happened to their servants when
she was travelling with her father.

Only his expert knowledge and hers had prevented
their wounds, from either a weapon or the thorns on
many of the desert shrubs, from becoming gangrenous
or deeply infected.

She had almost reached the bottom of the staircase
when a door just in front of her opened, and she felt her
heart give a leap as silhouetted against the light behind
him she saw the Earl.

He was wearing a long robe that reached to the
floor, and she realised he must have been awakened.

As Atayla walked towards him, she thought he was
staring at her incredulously. Then he asked, and his
voice was harsh:

"What is going on? What are you doing here, Miss
Lindsay?"

She parted her lips to explain to him, but he added
furiously:

"Need I ask? I saw the way you were behaving at
dinner and afterwards, but I could not believe you could
be so easily side-tracked from your main objective."

Atayla looked at him in astonishment, having no
idea what he was talking about.

Then, as if he suddenly lost control of his temper,
he reached out and, taking her by her arm, pulled her
through the open doorway into his bedroom.

She had a quick glimpse of a huge room with a light
burning beside an enormous four-poster bed, but she
could only think of the Earl's fingers, which hurt her,
while the furious expression on his face was frightening.

Never had she seen a man looking so angry, and
before she could speak, before she could think or ask
what he was doing, he said:

"I am well aware of why you came here, Miss

Lindsay, and why my wife sent you to seduce me into giving her the divorce she needs. But I did not expect you to behave like a prostitute with one of my guests."

"What are you . . . saying? How . . . dare you say such . . . things to . . . me?"

She could get no further, for the Earl went on in a voice that was almost a shout:

"Do you suppose I was deceived by my wife's sudden change of heart in returning my daughter to me? Do you suppose I am such a fool that I did not realise why she sent you and what your real mission was?"

He laughed mockingly.

"Only a man who was blind and deaf would believe you to be a Governess! Who ever heard of a Governess wearing Worth gowns, any one of which would have cost more than treble her year's salary?"

"I can . . . explain . . ." Atayla tried to say.

"There is nothing to explain," the Earl retorted. "You can go back to my wife and tell her that you have been unable to carry out your instructions. And, as far as I am concerned, you can take Felicity with you!"

"No! No!" Atayla cried. "I cannot do . . . that!"

"Why not?" the Earl asked. "Are you so anxious to stay?"

He looked down at her, and his eyes were hard as he went on:

"How boring you must have found it when I was not here for you to captivate! But you have certainly made up for it tonight, and I hope you have enjoyed yourself!"

"You must . . . listen to . . . me," Atayla pleaded. "Please . . . please . . . let me . . . explain!"

"I have no intention of listening to your lies," the Earl replied, "and you will, I am sure, try to make them more convincing than your very poor impersonation of a Governess."

He almost spat the words at her. Then, as if he was suddenly aware that she was trembling because she was frightened, that her eyes, which were looking up at him, were large in her small face, and her hair shimmering in the light of the candles was flecked with gold, he said in a very different tone:

"Perhaps it is cruel of me to send you away without anything to report. You came for one reason, and one reason only, and I would not wish you to be disappointed, unless of course you have had enough love-making for one night."

The words seemed to vibrate from him with a violence that he could not control.

As he finished speaking, his arms went round her, he pulled her against him, and his lips came down on hers.

He kissed her roughly and brutally, and although she tried to struggle against him, she was completely helpless in his arms.

As she tried with all her strength to push him away from her, she realised that he not only held her captive with his lips, but his arms were like bands of steel.

Suddenly he picked her up, and as she gave a cry of sheer terror he threw her down on the bed.

For a moment she could hardly believe what was happening. Then frantically she pleaded:

"Please . . . please . . . you are . . . frightening me! You . . . cannot do this . . . please . . . please . . . let me . . . go."

Her hands were free and she pushed violently against him and struggled to get up. Then as she gave another little scream of terror, he flung himself upon her and forced her backwards.

As he did so, he gripped her shoulder, his fingers digging into the wound she had received from the robber's dagger.

The pain of it struck through her body as if she had been stabbed again. She gave one little muffled scream at the agony of it, and knew nothing more. . . .

* * *

Atayla came back to consciousness from a darkness that seemed to envelop her, and not only was she unable to move but it was impossible to think.

Then she remembered that she was afraid, and made an inarticulate murmur of fear.

Something terrifying was happening, and she did not know what it was. She knew only that she was desperately frightened.

Then a deep voice which for the moment she could not recognise said:

"It is all right, nothing will hurt you now. Go to sleep."

Because it was a command and was easier to obey than refuse, she shut her eyes and slipped away into unconsciousness.

*　*　*

When Atayla woke again, she was aware that somebody was pulling back the curtains and the sunshine was coming in through the windows.

All she was aware of was a great disinclination to come back to reality, and she kept her eyes closed until she heard Jeannie moving about the room.

Then the maid asked in surprise:

"Are you all right, Miss? You didn't get into bed when you came back last night."

Atayla opened her eyes, and she could see Jeannie staring at her and realised she was lying on top of her bed, still wearing her negligé.

Everything that had happened came back like a flood-tide, but her memory stopped at the point when the agony of the Earl touching her wound had made her scream with pain.

What had happened after that was a blank.

Then she realised that she had not walked upstairs to her own room and the Earl must have carried her there, and she supposed she must have fainted and therefore not been aware of what was happening.

She knew Jeannie was waiting for an answer, and after a moment she said hesitatingly and in a voice that did not sound like her own:

"I was tired . . . when I got . . . back upstairs . . . and it was very . . . hot."

Jeannie turned from the bed.

"I were sorry to have to wake you, Miss, but I couldn't have bandaged Her Ladyship anything like as good as you did."

She put a brass can into the basin on the wash-hand-stand and covered it with a Turkish towel to keep it warm.

"You don't want to hurry to get up after such a disturbed night, Miss. I'll see to Her Ladyship."

"Thank you . . . Jeannie."

When Atayla was alone, she put her hand to her shoulder.

As she did so, she was aware that a frill of lace was slightly torn, and it must have happened when the Earl gripped her shoulder.

Then she remembered how he had kissed her and the things he had said, which still seemed wildly incomprehensible, until gradually as she thought back over what had happened they began to make sense.

Vaguely at the back of her mind she remembered that either her mother or her father had told her that for a woman to obtain a divorce in England, which was thought very reprehensible, however justified, she had to prove both infidelity on the part of her husband and, in addition, cruelty.

As the thought came to Atayla, she drew in her breath sharply, and understood why the Earl had insulted and raged at her.

"How could he . . . think such a . . . thing of . . . me?" she asked herself indignantly.

Then she supposed that it was her clothes, the beautiful gowns that the *Comtesse* had given her, which had made him believe she had been sent there to trap him into an act of immorality.

"It is . . . impossible!" she said aloud. "How could anybody believe . . . such a thing?"

Then, almost as if it were a picture in front of her eyes, she saw her reflection in the mirror and knew that last night, in the expensive, sequinned and embroidered gown of pale gold, she had looked, as Sir Christopher had said, like a ray of sunlight left over from the sunset.

Even so, no-one but the Earl, with his suspicions, his hatred, and his violence, could possibly believe her father's daughter could stoop to doing anything so utterly and completely despicable.

Then she remembered that to him she was not her father's daughter, but just an unknown woman who had arrived unexpectedly with a little girl who had been kidnapped by her mother.

It all seemed a tangled nightmare of horror from which it was impossible to extricate herself.

Suddenly she sat up in bed from sheer shock.

She remembered that when he had raged at her he had told her to leave.

After that, he had kissed her before throwing her down on the bed and frightening her to the point where she thought it would be impossible to escape from him.

She had to leave, but where could she go? And, what was more, she had no money.

The whole horror of it seemed to sweep over her like a wave that was drowning her, and it was impossible to breathe, impossible to survive.

Slowly, she got out of bed, knew that she was trembling, and found that she was unsteady on her legs.

She was not sure whether it was a result of last night's shock or because she now had a new and different terror to face.

It flashed through her mind that she might ask Sir Christopher for help.

Then she knew that after what the Earl had accused her of, she would rather die than approach his friend, even though they were, as he had said, distantly related.

"If I ask him for help, then the Earl will be more convinced than he is already that I am a wicked and immoral woman," she told herself.

It was difficult to believe that anybody would think such a thing of her!

Yet, with some intelligent part of her brain, she

began to understand how the Earl had reasoned it out from what she had to admit was circumstantial evidence, of a sort, against her.

He already suspected that she had come to the Castle to seduce him, and she had certainly allowed Sir Christopher to monopolise her all evening. The Earl had some grounds for being suspicious when he found her on the floor where his friend's bedroom was situated.

Atayla gave a little cry.

"It is horrible, beastly, degrading!" she told herself.

Yet, she felt despairingly she could in no way convince him that everything he believed was untrue.

'No wonder he hates me,' she thought, but she wondered why the Earl should think the *Comtesse* wanted a divorce when the *Comte*, according to Father Ignatius, was married with a wife in France.

It was all too complicated for Atayla to understand, and she went to the window, feeling in need of air because she felt shaky and as if she might faint again.

Then she told herself that she must get up and give Felicity breakfast.

With the greatest difficulty she managed to dress, thinking all the time that she would have to leave the Castle and not knowing how she could do so.

"You look done in, Miss!" Jeannie said when she came up to the Nursery. "Why don't you go and have a lie-down, and I'll look after Her Ladyship?"

"I am all right," Atayla replied. "But I wonder if you could arrange for Her Ladyship to ride with Jeb this morning? I have some things to do for myself."

"Yes, of course," Jeannie said. "I'll send one of the footmen to the stables now."

"I want to ride with you, Miss Lindsay," Felicity cried, looking up from her plate. "It is much more fun with you."

"Yes, I know, dearest," Atayla replied, "but I have a headache. So go with Jeb this morning, and perhaps when I feel better we can ride again this afternoon."

"That would be lovely!" Felicity said. "And I need not do any lessons?"

"Not this morning."

Atayla wanted to add: "And never with me again," but she knew it would upset the child, and she felt tears come into her eyes at the thought.

She did not want to leave the Castle, she wanted to stay, not only because it was a roof over her head but because she loved Felicity, and because everything about it had been exciting and different from anything she had ever known before.

She drank a cup of tea and felt a little better, but she knew it would be impossible to eat anything.

It was Jeannie who put Felicity's velvet riding-cap on her head, helped her into her jacket, and found her whip and gloves.

"I'll take her downstairs, Miss," she said, "and if you take my advice, you'll go to sleep for the next hour or two. No-one'll disturb you."

"Thank you," Atayla said weakly.

Felicity held up her face to be kissed.

"I will tell you all about it when I come back, Miss Lindsay, but it will not be such fun riding with Jeb as it would be racing with you."

"Do as Jeb tells you," Atayla admonished, "and be careful not to fall off, because that would worry me."

"I am a very good rider, like Papa," Felicity answered.

Then she was hurrying down the stairs with Jeannie, and Atayla went to her own bedroom.

She stood for a moment looking at the wardrobe that was overflowing with gowns and wondered how she would be able to pack everything and, when she was ready to leave the Castle, how far her money would take her.

Because she was trying to be practical, she took her handbag from the drawer and, opening it, found the purse which contained all the money that was left.

She emptied it out onto the white cover of the bed,

which had been made while they were having breakfast, and counted it.

There were three pound notes, two half-sovereigns, and three shillings. That was all that remained of the money which the *Comtesse* had given her in Tangiers.

Atayla stared at it despairingly, wondering how far away from the Castle it would take her and how she could live until she found work of some sort.

Now she wished she had made enquiries since she had been there as to how far away Baronswell in Northumberland was.

'Perhaps,' she thought, 'there will be some of Papa's relatives still living there.'

Because she had no idea of their names or ages, or even if they were still alive, she knew it would be much more difficult to arrive unannounced and unexpected in what had once been her grandfather's house than it had been to arrive at the Castle.

"What can I do? Where can I go?"

The questions seemed to be repeated tauntingly in the air round her, and she felt despairingly that she could not cope with life on her own. It would have been far better if the robber's dagger had killed her as the Arab had intended it should.

Then, as if she knew she had to do something, she opened a cupboard where she knew Jeannie had put some of the trunks, and found the smallest one, in which the things she had wanted for the journey from Tangiers had been packed.

She pulled it into the centre of the bedroom and opened it.

Then as she looked at the wardrobe packed with pretty gowns, and remembered that as many more were hanging up in the room next door, she knelt down on the floor beside the trunk, knowing it would be absurd to try to take everything with her, and she must pack just enough for her needs.

Yet, she had no idea what her needs would be, and she supposed it was because she was still feeling weak

and shaken from the events of the night before that as
the helplessness of her position once again swept over
her, tears gathered in her eyes.

She fought against them, but slowly, one by one,
they began to run down her cheeks, and it was too much
of an effort even to wipe them away.

She heard somebody come into the Nursery next
door and thought it was Jeannie returning from taking
Felicity to the stables.

She did not move, thinking the maid would not
disturb her, but as she stared through her tears at the
empty trunk in front of her, the door of her bedroom
opened.

She felt for her handkerchief, not wanting Jeannie
to ask why she was crying, then heard a deep voice ask:

"What are you doing?"

For a moment she thought she must be dreaming.

Then as she raised her eyes she saw not Jeannie
standing just inside the room, but the Earl.

He shut the door behind him and moved towards
her to stand looking down at her kneeling beside the
trunk, the tears on her cheeks.

"Why are you crying?" he asked.

She had the feeling that it was not what he had
intended to say, but because there seemed to be no
point in not answering him, she merely replied:

"I . . . I am . . . going . . . away."

As she spoke, she again felt in her belt for a
handkerchief. She did not seem to have one, and the
Earl took a handkerchief from his breast-pocket and held
it out to her.

After a moment she took it from him and wiped her
cheeks and eyes, wondering why he had come to her
bedroom and feeling that perhaps he was still as angry as
he had been the night before.

If he was, she felt it would be impossible to answer
his accusations, and yet she longed to tell him that he
had been mistaken.

He waited until she put the handkerchief into her lap. Then he said:

"I have come to apologise."

It was not what she had expected him to say, and her eyes widened as he went on:

"I learnt from Elizabeth Wick what you did for her last night. She is very grateful to you, and asks if before she leaves you will go and say good-bye to her."

"Y-yes . . . of course," Atayla managed to say.

"I have no excuse for the way I behaved," the Earl said, "except that you drove me mad with jealousy!"

Atayla felt she could not have heard him aright, and as she looked at him enquiringly, he said harshly:

"You have made me suffer in a million different ways ever since you came here, and last night, when I thought you had been with Hogarth, I could bear it no longer!"

"I . . . I do not think . . . understand," Atayla stammered.

Unexpectedly, the Earl smiled.

"Nor do I," he said. "It is something I have never experienced before, and I cannot explain it now."

He drew in his breath as he said:

"I suppose really I should ask you to tell me about yourself, and why you look as you do, and why you are dressed from Paris. Instead, I can only say that you have frightened me ever since you arrived."

"F-frightened you?" Atayla questioned in a little voice that seemed to come from very far away.

She was not certain what was happening.

She only knew that just as last night seemed a terrifying, dark nightmare, so now she seemed to have stepped into a dream that filled the room with sunshine and made her heart beat in a very strange and incomprehensible manner.

"If you really are, as I accused you last night, working on behalf of my wife, to incriminate me so that she can obtain a divorce, I know now that it does not matter. Whoever you are, whatever you are doing here, you are still you, and that is something from which I cannot escape."

"What . . . what are you . . . saying to me?" Atayla asked in a whisper.

The Earl drew in his breath.

"I am saying," he said, "that strangely, unpredictably, and completely incomprehensibly, I have fallen in love with you, and although I can hardly believe it myself, there is nothing I can do about it!"

"It . . . cannot be . . . true!"

"It is true!" he said. "And that is my only excuse for the way I treated you and the things I said."

He smiled, and it was very beguiling.

"I now come back to my original question—will you forgive me?"

A little unsteadily Atayla rose to her feet.

As she did so, she found it impossible to take her eyes from the Earl's, and she stood in front of him, looking up at him, as she said:

"I do not think I am . . . hearing what you are saying to me. Perhaps I am just . . . dreaming . . . and this is not . . . real."

The Earl moved a little nearer to her.

"It is very real," he said, "so real that nothing else matters, except that you are here. If you think I will let you leave, you are very much mistaken!"

"Y-you told me to . . . go," Atayla said childishly.

"Only because you tortured me until I could bear it no longer!" he answered. "Can you imagine what I felt when I saw you walking down the corridor? I believed . . ."

"How . . . could you . . . believe such wicked things of me?" Atayla interrupted.

"I asked myself the same question when I learnt where in fact you had been," the Earl admitted. "At the same time, I have been trying to hate and despise you ever since you first arrived, but have found it impossible."

Atayla looked at him wide-eyed, trying to realise

exactly what he was saying to her. Then in a different tone of voice the Earl said:

"Help me, make me understand, tell me exactly why you came here with Felicity."

"I . . . wanted to tell you . . . last night . . . but you would not listen."

"I know," the Earl said, "and when I carried you back here unconscious and I saw the wound in your shoulder, I found it impossible to go on believing you were anything but as pure, sweet, and honest as you look."

He put out his hand to Atayla and said:

"Trust me. Tell me the truth, and whatever it may be, I know it will not prevent me from continuing to love you."

Without thinking, because his hands were outstretched towards her, Atayla put her fingers in his, and as she touched him she felt as if a streak of sunshine swept through her body.

She knew it was because he thrilled her, and although she had tried to hate him as he had tried to hate her, what she felt for him now was very different.

It was not only that he was handsome, magnificent, and she liked to look at him even when he was scowling at her, but also that when he had gone away from the Castle it had seemed empty.

Although she would not admit it to herself, she had missed him and longed for his return.

Last night, even while she had been talking to Sir Christopher about her father, she had been vividly conscious of the Earl seated at the top of the table.

She had thought he looked Royal, but more than that he had looked a man she could admire because he was indeed a man, and she could feel the vibrations from him even when she was not looking at him.

Now as her fingers tightened on his, she was so vividly conscious of him that she felt they were joined together by some invisible link, and there was no necessity for explanations.

She belonged to him, but how, she did not dare to think even to herself. She just knew, because he was touching her, that she was a part of him.

Then as she raised her eyes, she knew that he was thinking the same thing.

He took his hands from hers, and very slowly, as if he was afraid to frighten her, he put his arms round her and drew her closer to him.

"There is really no need to say anything," he said. "All I know is that I love you very much, my darling, and you are mine, and nothing else is of any importance."

His voice was very deep and moving as he spoke. Then, still slowly and gently, his lips found hers.

He kissed her in a very different way from the way he had the night before, and as she felt the tenderness of his kiss, her heart seemed to turn over in her breast.

She knew this was love as she had wanted to find it, the love that her father had had for her mother, and which was the only treasure that was of any importance.

The Earl drew her closer still, and his lips became more demanding, more insistent, and very possessive, and yet he was still very gentle, and because it was so wonderful, Atayla felt once again the tears come into her eyes and run down her cheeks.

He raised his head.

"My darling, you must not cry. The goblins are all gone, and they will not frighten you again."

She tried to smile at what he had said. Then, because it was too much to bear, she hid her face against his shoulder.

"I . . . I thought I should . . . have to go away and . . . l-leave you!" she whispered.

His arms tightened.

"That is something you will never do. I was crazy last night when I told you to go, when I knew I could not live without you."

Suddenly he stiffened and said:

"You know, much as I love you, my precious one, I

cannot, at the moment, ask you to marry me. But I will give Nadine the divorce she wants."

Atayla raised her head.

"You do not . . . really believe I came here with such wicked . . . intentions?"

"Why did you come?"

"It is so much less . . . complicated than what you have been . . . thinking," Atayla replied. "The *Comtesse*, for that is what she is called in Tangiers, asked Father Ignatius, at whose Mission I was staying, if he knew of an Englishwoman who would take Felicity safely to England."

She saw that the Earl was listening intently, but his arms were still holding her.

"I had been very ill," Atayla continued, "after desert robbers had swooped on our caravan . . . killed my father . . . and stabbed . . . me."

"So that is how you received that terrible wound on your shoulder!" the Earl exclaimed. "When I saw it last night, I understood why you fainted when I touched it."

"It had only just healed," Atayla replied. "As I had no money and could not stay at the Mission indefinitely, Father Ignatius took me to the Villa where Felicity's mother was living, and the very next day we started our journey to England."

"But why—why did my wife suddenly decide to return the child to me after taking her away in that cruel and heartless manner?" the Earl enquired.

"The *Comtesse* is very ill," Atayla replied, "and she said that Felicity was upsetting her relationship with the *Comte*. Moreover, the child herself was not . . . happy with him."

She felt the Earl stiffen and was afraid he might abuse the *Comte* as he had before, but he did not speak, and she went on:

"I agreed because I wanted to get back to England and try to find my relations, and it was a wonderful opportunity to have everything paid."

She looked towards the bed as she said:

"When we arrived, we had spent everything that I was given for the journey, and that is all I have left."

The Earl gave a little laugh that was very tender.

"And you really thought, my precious, that you could leave me and manage on your own with only that much between you and starvation?"

"I . . . I was frightened," Atayla confessed.

"You will never be frightened again," he promised. "Now I understand, and again I beg you to forgive me for thinking you had an ulterior motive when you arrived here looking so exquisitely beautiful, and of course so unsuitably dressed."

He paused before he said:

"I can guess now, and it was extremely stupid of me not to have thought of it before, but of course it was my wife who gave you the clothes you have been wearing."

Atayla nodded.

"The robbers took literally everything Papa and I possessed. All I had to wear was a Mission dress of grey cotton, which was so ugly that I am sure nobody would have looked at me except in horror!"

The Earl laughed.

"However ugly your dress, it would not hide your hair, your eyes, your adorable little nose, or your lips, my precious one, which were made for my kisses."

He kissed her again, demandingly, passionately. Then he asked:

"How many men have kissed you in the past?"

"None," Atayla replied, "and actually . . . I have never . . . met a man like . . . you before."

"I shall try to prevent you from meeting any men like me again," the Earl said. "But what on earth were you talking about to Christopher last night when I imagined he was making love to you?"

Atayla laughed.

"He knew all about Papa, and had read his books and the articles he wrote for the *Royal Geographical Magazine*."

The Earl looked down at her in surprise. Then he said:

"Are you telling me that your father was Gordon Lindsay?"

"Yes, but I never thought you would have heard of him."

"I have heard of him," the Earl said, "because I happen to be the President of the Royal Geographical Society, and naturally I read the magazine whenever it is published."

"How could I have imagined . . . how could I have guessed that you would have . . . heard of Papa?"

"I found his articles extremely interesting and exciting," the Earl said, "but not as interesting and exciting as I find his daughter!"

Then he was kissing her again, kissing her with long, slow kisses which seemed to Atayla to take her heart from between her lips and make it his.

Because everything was suddenly so wonderful and so perfect, she moved a little closer to him, and he kissed her for a long time before he said:

"Now, as this is the first time you have been kissed and I am the only man to do so, tell me what you feel."

"It is wonderful! There are no . . . words," Atayla replied. "Your kisses are like the stars over the desert when they seem to fill not only the sky but the Universe and the sunshine coming up over the horizon. It is happiness I cannot possibly express . . . except perhaps in music."

The rapture and the touch of passion in her voice made the Earl draw in his breath.

Then he was kissing her until the room seemed to swing dizzily round them and he was lifting her into the sky, where there was only sunshine, and it seemed to burn in them both until it became a fire.

"I love you . . . I love you!" Atayla said first in her heart, then out loud.

"And I love you, my darling," he said, "but there is a great deal to do before I can make you my wife."

"I am not quite . . . sure that you should . . . marry me."

"I am quite sure, and I intend to marry you!" the Earl said firmly. "Nothing and nobody shall stop me, but as you must be aware, my precious one, a divorce takes time, and it also causes a scandal, which is extremely regrettable from the point of view of the family, but there is nothing we can do about that."

Because she loved him, Atayla heard the note of regret in his voice, and knew how much he would hate his private affairs to be dragged through the mud.

Then, as if he told himself that nothing mattered except their love, he swept her into his arms and was kissing her again.

It was impossible to think, but only to feel that unexpectedly, miraculously, they had reached a Heaven where there were no problems but only love.

Chapter Seven

Having gone through the day still in the dream-world into which the Earl had taken her, all the time she was with Felicity Atayla was counting the hours, the minutes, and the seconds until she could be with him again.

After having lost time and space with the wonder of their love, the Earl had said in a voice that sounded strange and unsteady:

"I must leave you, my darling. The Wicks are leaving after luncheon and so is Hogarth. Although I know now I need not be jealous of him, I still do not want you to see him again."

"When can we be . . . together?" Atayla asked.

"I think it would be best after tea," the Earl said. "I am sure you can leave somebody to amuse Felicity and come down to my Sitting-Room, where we can make plans."

She smiled at him, and he thought that the whole room was lit from the wonder in her eyes.

"I have a great deal to tell you," he said in a deep voice. "At the same time, all that matters is that you love me and I will never lose you."

He kissed her quickly, as if he knew that if he lingered he would never be able to go. Then he had gone from her bedroom, shutting the door behind him.

For the moment Atayla could not move, then she ran to the window, as if only by looking up at the sky could she be certain that the darkness had gone, she was no longer afraid, and could thank God for her happiness.

When Felicity returned from riding, they had luncheon, and afterwards, because Atayla knew she had to fill the afternoon, she made Felicity lie on the sofa and read to her one of the books she had brought up from the Library.

It was about Africa, but soon Atayla felt that she could explain to Felicity what she knew about it so much better in her own words.

So she told stories of the desert, the Arab tribes, and the strange towns, like Fez and Marrakesh, which had remained practically unchanged through the centuries.

Because she was so happy where she was now, the past seemed to Atayla to be receding into the distance, and the only things that were real were the Earl and the Castle.

At three o'clock she took Felicity riding again, and as she did not want the child to be tired, they did not gallop or race, but only rode round the Park and in the orchards.

Because of her love, Atayla felt the grounds were even more beautiful than they had been before and meant something so precious that it was part of her heart and her mind.

As if the child knew perceptively what she was thinking, Felicity asked:

"You like the Castle, do you not, Miss Lindsay?"

"It is the most beautiful place I have ever seen," Atayla answered, "and you and I are going to try to make it as beautiful inside as it is outside."

Felicity put her head on one side, as if she was thinking. Then she said:

"Do you mean with love?"

"Yes," Atayla answered, "with love. Then it will be perfect!"

When Felicity had had tea, Atayla felt her heart

beating more quickly because it was now only a question
of minutes before she would see the Earl.

She started to play a game with the little girl, with
her dolls' house, and they rearranged the rooms and the
small dolls which fitted inside it, and she told her a story
about each one of them, so that they became like real
people.

When at five o'clock Jeannie came to the Nursery as
Atayla had asked her to do, she said:

"Here I am, Miss, and as I guessed Her Ladyship
would be playing with the dolls' house, Chef has made
some tiny little dishes which can be put inside for the
dolls to eat."

Felicity was entranced at this idea, and while she
and Jeannie were arranging them, Atayla slipped away.

She paused just for a moment in her own bedroom
to look at herself in the mirror and wonder if the gown
she was wearing was one of her most becoming.

But she knew as she looked at her reflection that it
was the radiance in her eyes that the Earl would see, and
the softness of her lips.

She blushed as she thought of him kissing her, and
she knew it was something she wanted more than
anything else in the world.

Because she was in such a hurry to be with him, she
ran down the stairs, along the corridor, and down the
Grand Staircase to the Hall.

The footman on duty moved towards her, but
without waiting Atayla ran on towards the Earl's private
Sitting-Room and opened the door herself.

As she expected, he was waiting for her, standing
with his back to the mantelpiece, and as she entered
their eyes met, and for the moment it was impossible for
either of them to move.

Atayla felt as if her whole being vibrated towards
him, and as if he felt the same he held out his arms and
she ran to him.

He held her very close against him but he did not
kiss her, and after a moment he said in a very deep voice:

"Before I tell you how much I love you, my precious one, I think we should talk. There are a great many things you must know and many explanations to be made."

Because his arms were round her and she could feel his heart beating against hers, it was hard to listen to what he was saying.

Yet, her mind told her that he was being sensible and she must do as he asked.

He pressed his lips for a moment against her forehead, then drew her to the sofa. They sat down side by side and he took her hand in his.

"This is the room in which I first saw you," he said, "and because you were so beautiful, I was sure you were dangerous, and I fought not only against you but against my own instinct."

"I can understand that now," Atayla said, "but you were very . . . intimidating."

"I swear that I will never frighten you again! And try to understand that if you were frightened, so was I!"

She looked up at him, and with a smile he said:

"After all I had been through, I had sworn that never again would I give any woman my heart—never again would I be such a fool as to fall in love."

Because Atayla knew that his first love had been the *Comtesse,* she felt a little stab of jealousy, and looked down so that he would not be aware of what she was feeling.

He gave a little laugh that was very tender as he said:

"Yes, I was in love with Nadine, but it was not in the least, my precious one, what I feel now for you. I thought I loved her because she was so beautiful, and also because her parents told me she wished to marry me. When I asked her, she said the same thing."

He paused, but Atayla did not speak, and he went on:

"It is difficult now to realise how trusting I was, and perhaps conceited enough to think that while I was what is called a 'Matrimonial Catch,' Nadine really loved me as a man."

There was a bitter note in his voice which made Atayla tighten her fingers on his.

"Why did she not love you?"

Even as she asked the question she thought it extraordinary that anybody as handsome, wealthy, and important as the Earl would not arouse love in a young girl who could not have had much experience of men.

Once again he read her thoughts and said:

"When she married me, Nadine was already passionately in love with the *Comte* de Soisson!"

"Oh . . . no!" Atayla exclaimed. "Why then did she not marry him?"

"He was already married," the Earl answered, "and had been for some years. The French marry young. It was an arranged marriage, and his wife has an equally distinguished lineage as that of the de Soissons."

"And you did not know?"

"I had not the slightest idea she had even met the man," the Earl answered, "until after we were married, when we encountered him by chance at a party in London."

There was silence for a few moments, as if he was looking back over the past. Then he said:

"Only a complacent man, or an idiot, would not have been aware that the moment my wife saw de Soisson she seemed to come alive, and the expression on their faces as they looked at each other was very revealing."

"It must have been very hurtful for you."

"I was hurt because, although I knew by that time that Nadine did not love me, she was at least pleasant and complacent and did everything I asked of her. She was also carrying our child."

There was silence until Atayla asked:

"What happened?"

"Nothing then," the Earl replied. "I asked my wife to tell me the truth, and she finally admitted that she was in love with the *Comte*. After a great deal of prevarication and lies, she told me that she had loved him ever since she was seventeen, and that he had seduced her when she was in Paris with her parents."

Atayla gave a little cry of horror, and the Earl went on:

"The *Comte* had then withdrawn from what he knew was an explosive situation and told Nadine he would not see her again. But soon after Felicity was born I became aware that they were writing to each other and meeting secretly whenever he came to London."

"What did you do . . . about it?"

I threatened to kill him, and he was wise enough to keep out of my way. But Nadine made it very clear where her affections lay, and we became more and more estranged, until we saw as little as possible of each other, except on public occasions or when we had guests staying in the Castle."

Because she could not bear to think of him being unhappy, Atayla murmured softly:

"It must have been very . . . hard for . . . you."

"I told myself I did not care," the Earl answered, "and actually I no longer loved Nadine. But she was my wife, and I was determined that there would be no scandal which would hurt the family and damage our name, which has been respected for centuries."

"I can understand how that sort of life must have made you very . . . very . . . unhappy."

"I suppose I grew bitter and cynical," the Earl said, "and I told myself that all women were untrustworthy and promiscuous."

Atayla shivered, and the Earl said:

"All that is now forgotten, my precious. I know you are different, so very, very different, and are everything I wanted to find in the woman I loved but I was sure did not exist."

Because what he had said moved her and the note of passion in his voice made her yearn for his kisses,

Atayla turned her face up to his and thought he would take her in his arms.

Then, with what seemed a superhuman effort, he looked away from her as he said:

"I must go on telling you everything that happened so that you will understand."

"I do . . . understand," Atayla said. "At the same time . . . I am . . . listening."

"Three years ago," the Earl said, "I learnt that the *Comte* was in England and Nadine was seeing him, and I was quite certain they were lovers even though she deceived me so cleverly that I could not prove it."

His lips tightened before he said:

"We had some flaming rows, then one day, quite unexpectedly, when I was out hunting, she left the Castle early in the morning, and it was not until I returned just before dinner that I learnt that she had gone and had taken Felicity with her."

"It was a . . . cruel thing to do."

"I am sure it was the *Comte*'s idea, because he hated me and wanted to hurt me," the Earl said simply. "It was not surprising, as I had said some very unpleasant things about him to Nadine, which she doubtless repeated to him."

"What did you do?"

"When I realised she and the *Comte* had left England together and gone to Paris, I did nothing."

"Nothing?"

"At first I pretended that she had gone on a holiday with the child and would soon be returning. Then, as the months passed and people began to talk, I refused to discuss it, and left them to think what they wished."

"And you did not hear from . . . your wife?"

"I heard nothing," the Earl replied, "until about ten months ago. Then a letter arrived from some French Solicitors, informing me that the *Comte*'s wife was dead, and asking me to divorce my wife so that she and de Soisson could be married."

"So the *Comte*'s wife is dead!" Atayla exclaimed in surprise. "Father Ignatius was not aware of that."

"Yes, he was free to marry, but Nadine was still tied to me."

"And you would not divorce her?"

"Why should I?" the Earl asked. "A divorce, whoever is at fault, causes a scandal, and what is a private affair between two people then becomes public and is reported in the newspapers for every Tom, Dick, and Harry to read."

"So you refused."

"I refused categorically, and had no wish whatever to remarry, until, my darling, I saw you."

"How could I have guessed . . . how could I have thought for one moment that you could ever love me," Atayla asked, "when all I could see was hate in your eyes?"

"I was hating you because you disturbed and upset me; because every time I looked at you, my heart seemed to turn a dozen somersaults."

He smiled before he went on:

"I was convinced that you were a temptress, a serpent, who had been sent to blackmail me into giving Nadine a divorce."

"I do not think I . . . understand," Atayla said.

"It is quite simple," the Earl answered. "If she could obtain evidence against me of infidelity, and since we had so many rows before she left she could call the servants as witnesses to my cruelty towards her, she would definitely have a case against me."

He paused for a moment, then went on:

"Actually, I thought that she would more probably insist that I divorce her, citing the *Comte*. The case would then go through much more quickly and with less publicity."

"I . . . understand," Atayla said, "but will you . . . now divorce her . . . as she . . . wants?"

"I have already draughted a letter to my Solicitors in London," the Earl replied, "telling them to go ahead immediately and to inform my wife that she will be free as quickly as it can be arranged."

As he finished speaking, he released Atayla's hand and put his arms round her.

"Then, my precious love," he said, "I will be able to ask you to do me the honour of becoming my wife."

"You know it will be the most . . . wonderful thing that could ever . . . happen to . . . me," Atayla said.

"I swear I will make you happy! I do not think either of us doubts that. But, my darling, it means that you will have to leave here immediately."

Atayla sifffened and looked at him in astonishment.

"Leave?" she asked. "But . . . why?"

"Because, my sweet, if I am to be what is called the innocent party, it would be a great mistake for you to stay here, even with Grandmama as a Chaperone."

"But . . . why? Why?" Atayla asked again.

"Because in England we have a faceless official called 'The Queen's Proctor,' and whoever brings a case for divorce has to lead a blameless life until the case has been heard and a further six months have passed."

"Six months!" Atayla exclaimed, with a little cry of dismay.

"It will be hard, very hard, but then we will be together for the rest of our lives."

"I cannot . . . lose you," Atayla said. "I cannot bear to . . . leave you!"

"Oh, my darling, if you only knew what it means to me to hear you say that," the Earl replied. "But it is something that has to be done, first because I must protect you not only against any scandal and gossip but also against myself, and secondly, I must be free!"

He gave a little laugh as he added:

"Do you really think I could be here with you every day in the Castle without making everybody aware how much I love you and how desperately I want you?"

Atayla knew he was speaking sense. At the same time, she was afraid to leave him.

"Suppose," she said, "if it takes all that long . . .

time for you to be . . . free, you find when it is . . . all over that you do not . . . love me?"

"That will never happen," the Earl answered. "I love you, adore you, and worship you. I also know unmistakably that we not only belong to each other but that nothing and nobody will ever come between us."

As if he thought he was being too confident, he put his fingers under Atayla's chin and turned her face up to his.

"Swear to me," he said, "that you love me as I love you, and that no other man will ever mean anything to you."

"There is . . . no other man in the whole world but you," Atayla replied, "and it is only because I love you so desperately with all my heart and soul that I am afraid of losing you."

The Earl pulled her closer and his lips were on hers.

Then as she surrendered herself to the insistent demand of his kisses, she knew he was right when he said they could never be parted and they belonged to each other.

Once again she felt as if the sunshine swept through her, lighting her whole body and kindling a fire within her which answered the fire she felt burning within the Earl.

It was in the beat of their hearts, in the touch of their lips, and in every breath they drew.

Only as he carried her up into the sky and they touched the wings of ecstasy did she say a little incoherently:

"I love you . . . I love you . . . and when you kiss me there is . . . nothing but love . . . and you in the whole world!"

The Earl kissed her again, and she knew they were no longer human but part of the stars, the moon, and the sun, and it would be impossible ever to come back to earth.

* * *

"I love you!" the Earl said a long time later, and his

voice was deep and unsteady, "but, my precious, I have to tell you what plans I am making for you."

"What are . . . they?" Atayla asked, and now she was afraid because his voice was serious.

"I have an aunt who lives about five miles from here. She is a widow and a very kind woman given to good works. I know she is lonely, because she has no children, and that she would welcome both you and Felicity if you went to live with her."

"I shall be . . . able to see . . . you?" Atayla asked.

The Earl smiled.

"You may be quite certain of that. I will ride across the fields and we will meet several times a week, and naturally you will bring Felicity here to see her great-grandmother."

"You are . . . quite sure you will . . . come?" Atayla asked in a small voice.

"You may be sure of it!" the Earl replied. "At the same time, it will be hard, my darling, as you are well aware, not to be with you every moment of the day and night. But we have to wait. Then when finally we are together, we shall be able to forget the discomfort and misery we must endure so that we can be married."

"You are . . . certain that is really the . . . quickest way of doing it?"

"It is the only way," the Earl replied. "In fact, if my wife brought a divorce case against me, because she has already left me and is living in what the world calls 'sin,' she would probably not be successful in the Courts, and we would have to remain married for the rest of our lives."

Atayla gave a cry of horror, and the Earl went on:

"Do not be afraid—that is not going to happen! But because I am fighting in every way for our future happiness, we have to observe the proprieties and be very, very careful."

"I will do whatever you tell me to do."

The Earl looked down at her and his eyes were very tender.

"You are so sweet, my lovely one," he said, "and one day, when you are my wife, I shall be able to tell you how much you mean to me, and give you all the things I long for you to have."

"All I want are . . . your kisses."

As she spoke she saw the fire in the Earl's eyes, and he kissed her until they were both breathless.

Only when it was possible to speak again did she ask:

"How soon . . . are Felicity and I to . . . leave?"

"I shall arrange everything tomorrow," he said, "and I anticipate that my aunt will be ready to receive you the following day."

He saw the unhappiness in Atayla's eyes and said:

"That gives us two nights and a day together, my precious love. Will you dine with me tonight?"

"Can I do that?"

"Nobody as yet knows of our plans, and although perhaps some of the staff will be surprised that a Governess should come downstairs to the Dining-Room, I think if anyone asks questions in the future, they will be loyal to us. Besides, as I have already said, you are chaperoned by my grandmother."

"You are going to tell her about us?"

"I will not have to tell her," the Earl replied. "I do not mind betting a very large sum that she already knows what is happening."

He saw the consternation in Atayla's face and laughed.

"Do not worry! Grandmama will be so delighted that I am to be married again and have an heir that she will welcome any woman, and especially you, my precious one."

"Why should you think that?"

"Because she already admires you, and although she is suspicious that you are not the Governess you pretend to be, she will, I know, be very impressed when she learns who your father was."

"Are you saying that she will have heard of Papa?"

"Why does that seem so surprising to you? I am only astonished that she has not discovered it already!" the Earl said. "Grandmama visited North Africa several times with my grandfather, who was an inveterate traveller and insatiably curious about the strange customs of the Moslem and Arab world."

Atayla gave a little cry.

"It is so extraordinary! Papa had no idea anybody ever read his books except some elderly Dons in Universities and a few younger students who study the subject in Schools. And yet, here, where I least expected it, I find that not only you and Sir Christopher but also your grandmother have heard of him!"

"Which is the most important?" the Earl asked.

"You, of course!" Atayla answered, resting her cheek against his shoulder. "I am so thrilled, and so proud that you realise how clever Papa was, and how valuable in the future his research on African tribes will be to those who really want to know about that almost-unknown Continent."

"I will make sure that your father's books are known, and when I next go to London I will persuade his publishers to take such steps that the sales will be much larger than they anticipate."

"That is the most wonderful present you could give me!" Atayla cried. "Thank you . . . thank you for being so . . . understanding."

The Earl did not answer. He only kissed her again.

Then as she realised that the time they had been together had flown and she should go upstairs and say good-night to Felicity, Atayla rose to her feet.

"I may really dine with you this evening?"

"I have no intention of sitting in the Dining-Room alone," the Earl said, "and also, my precious, we have a great deal to say to each other after dinner, only perhaps it will not all be in words."

His eyes were on her lips, and she felt as if he kissed them again.

Then, because she wanted to stay but knew she

should go, she smiled at him and went from the room before he could prevent her from doing so.

As she went upstairs, she was saying over and over again in her heart a prayer of gratitude and thankfulness for the happiness she had found so unexpectedly at a moment when she had been feeling nothing but fear and misery.

* * *

Felicity had had her supper and was undressed and ready for bed when Atayla came into the Nursery.

"You are back!" Felicity cried. "I have so much to tell you! Jeannie and I put the dishes in the dolls' house and they had such a big supper that we think they will all have tummy-aches."

"I hope that is something that will not happen to you," Atayla said.

"No, of course not," Felicity replied. "I must not have a tummy-ache because tomorrow you promised to race me on my pony. Did you ask Papa if he would race too?"

"I am sure he will want to," Atayla answered, and Felicity gave a little shout of joy.

"I love Papa when he is racing with me," she said, "and when those silly people have gone away, perhaps he will race every day."

Atayla felt a little constriction of her heart at the thought that the Earl would not be with them and she and Felicity would be living in a strange house.

However, she did not want to spoil the evening by thinking about it, so she heard Felicity's prayers and kissed her good-night.

Felicity put her arms round her neck and kissed her.

"I love you, Miss Lindsay," she said, "and I am loving everybody like you told me to do."

She thought for a moment, then she said:

"I love you, and Papa, and Grandmama because she lets me play with her jewellery, and Jeannie and Jackson, and of course *Dragonfly* but not quite as much as I love you."

Atayla laughed.

"Thank you, darling, that is a very big compliment."

Felicity kissed her again. Then Atayla tucked her up and said:

"Good-night, dearest. God keep you, and His angels watch over you."

It was something her mother had said to her as a child, and as she left Felicity's room she thought that God had watched over her and sent His angels to protect her and help her.

Now never again in her whole life would she doubt that help was always there if one prayed for it.

Jeannie had her bath ready for her, and they had a long discussion as to which gown would be most suitable for her to wear as she was dining downstairs.

Because she thought the Earl would think it wise, Atayla told Jeannie for the first time about her father and how he had written articles for the *Royal Geographical Magazine* and how the Earl had read them because he was President of the Society.

"You can understand," she said, "that it is very exciting for me to find here in the Castle somebody who understands the work my father was doing in Africa."

"Well, whatever the reason, I thinks it's ever so nice for you, Miss, to be dining downstairs, which is where you ought to be. We were all saying in the Housekeeper's room that you looked prettier than any of the other ladies who came to the party."

"Thank you," Atayla said with a smile.

The gown they decided on was white and silver and made her look very young, which was how she felt the Earl would want her to look, young and untouched by anybody except himself.

When she was ready, she stood for a moment looking in the mirror. Her eyes were shining with excitement, and she thought perhaps the Earl was wise in sending her away.

It would have been impossible for anybody who saw them together not to be aware that they were in love.

"I love him, I love him!" she told her reflection, then walked excitedly to the door.

Only as she reached it did Jeannie, who was gathering up her things, say:

"Oh, by the way, Miss, I nearly forgot, there's a letter come for you by the afternoon post. I put it on the mantelpiece so you'd see it when you came up to the Nursery."

"A letter?" Atayla questioned.

"Yes, Miss, with a foreign stamp on it, but you went straight into Her Ladyship's bedroom, so I expects you missed it."

Atayla did not speak, but she went into the Nursery and found the letter where Jeannie had put it on the mantelpiece propped up against the clock.

She looked at it and saw as she had expected that it had come from Tangiers, and she wondered if it was from the *Comtesse*.

Just for a moment she thought it might be a mistake to open it. Perhaps something she might read there would spoil her evening with the Earl.

Then she knew she could not go down to him and be wondering all the time whether there was news of his wife which was important to them both.

Slowly, because her fingers were trembling, she opened the envelope.

There was only a very thin sheet of writing-paper inside, and as she drew it out she read the signature and was aware that it was not from the *Comtesse* but from Father Ignatius.

She thought it was kind of him to write, and started to read what he had written in his upright, well-formed hand.

My dear Atayla,
    I am praying that God has brought you safely to the end of your journey and that you

*are now installed in Roth Castle and the Earl
has been pleased to see his daughter again and
have her with him.*

*I am writing to give you the very sad news
that the Comtesse died yesterday and her
Funeral will take place tomorrow.*

*She had, as the Doctors suspected, a
deeply infected lung, and there was no chance
of her ever recovering from the Tuberculosis
which, alas, takes the lives of so many people,
and for which there is no known cure.*

*I am hoping you will break the news of her
mother's death to Felicity as gently as possible,
who we know loved her and was loved by her.
But she is now with her father, and I think
God, in his wisdom, directed that she should
reach England in safety before this tragedy
happened.*

*Write to me when you have the time. You
know that I pray for you daily, that God is
looking after you, and His love never fails.*

> *I remain, my dear Atayla,*
> *Yours in Christ Jesus,*
> *Father Ignatius*

Atayla reread the letter and for a moment she could
hardly believe that what she had read was not just a
figment of her imagination and her hopes.

To make sure, she read it again.

Then as she put it back into the envelope, she knew
that Father Ignatius was right: God had looked after her
and the future was filled with sunshine.

* * *

The Earl looked down at Atayla and said gently:
"I think, my darling, we should leave now."
"Yes, of course," Atayla answered.
As she spoke she found it difficult to believe that
she was the Earl's wife and they were leaving the Castle

to join the private train that was waiting for them at the Halt.

They had been married in the little Church in the Park, and the only other person there had been a wildly excited Felicity, who had been allowed to be a bridesmaid and hold Atayla's bouquet when the Earl put the ring on her finger.

It was a very simple, very quiet little Service, but the sincerity of it seemed to Atayla to join with the music that vibrated from her heart to the Earl's and was the song of the angels in a special Heaven into which he was taking her.

"How could I have known, how could I have guessed," she asked, "when I came here frightened and with no money, that I was stepping into Paradise? Or that the Earl of Rothwell, who threatened to throw Felicity and me out into the night, was the man I would love with all my heart and soul?"

As soon as the Earl read Father Ignatius's letter, he had taken control of the situation. He insisted that they should be married at once, secretly and without any fuss.

The explanation of what had happened to Nadine, he said, could be given after they returned from their honeymoon.

"Will people not think it very . . . strange that you should marry me?" Atayla asked.

"Some of my friends and relations will obviously ask questions," the Earl said, "but as far as the Social World is concerned, Nadine has not been heard of or mentioned for three years. They will, I expect, assume that she died before Felicity came back to the Castle, and as a free man I can obviously do what I like."

He gave a laugh before he said:

"And what I like, my precious one, is that you should be my wife and we will be together now, at this moment, and forever!"

He kissed from her lips any further questions she might ask, and she knew that all she wanted was to be in his arms and not have to worry ever again about the future.

The Dowager, as the Earl had expected, had been delighted.

"You are certainly full of surprises, my child," she had said to Atayla, "but I was always convinced you were not the Governess you pretended to be."

"I only wish you could have met Papa before he died," Atayla replied. "I am sure he would have interested and amused you far better than I can."

"I am just staying alive now," the Dowager said, "to see Valor's son running about the Castle, and then I can give half my jewellery to him, and half to Felicity."

"It would be a great mistake for you to spoil them," the Earl replied, "and you must keep alive so that your great-grandson can enjoy you just as I always have done."

The Dowager was delighted.

"I thought I was growing too old for compliments," she said, "but I am hoping to hear some more before I finally sink into the grave."

They had laughed, then she had kissed Atayla and the Earl and said:

"Go off and enjoy yourselves. I will look after the Castle until you come back."

"And I will look after you, Grandmama," Felicity said. "I am going to be very, very good, so as not to worry my new Mama, whom I love very much."

Because she was so moved by what the child said, Atayla felt the tears come into her eyes, and, as if the Earl understood, he put his arm round her.

"We are not going to worry about anything," he said, "and Felicity is going to look after the horses for us, are you not, my poppet?"

He picked her up in his arms as he spoke, and Felicity hugged him and said:

"I'll look after them and see that Jackson exercises them properly so that you'll be pleased when you come back."

"I will be very, very pleased," the Earl said with a smile, and kissed her.

As he did so, Atayla thought it was the first time she had seen him kiss his daughter, and the love he gave Felicity would be the same as the love he would give their children.

"I was right," she told herself. "All the Castle needed was love, and now it will be perfect!"

The household was waiting on the steps to wave them off, and Atayla and the Earl, having said good-bye to Mr. Osborne and Dawson, walked down the steps to where the carriage was waiting.

Felicity threw the first rose-petals at them. Then there was a shower of petals and also some rice, which Atayla remembered symbolised fertility.

There were cheers as the carriage drove down the drive, and Atayla slipped her hand into the Earl's.

"Did you enjoy your wedding, my precious?" he asked. "To me it was exactly the ceremony I wanted to have with somebody I love, and the Church seemed to be filled with love."

"That is . . . what I felt too."

He lifted her hand to his lips as he said:

"I knew that was what you were feeling! I think I know everything about you, and while I read your thoughts, I know they are my thoughts too."

"Oh, darling, you must always be like that!" Atayla said. "And I love you until I can only think, dream, and speak of love!"

* * *

Later that night, when the Earl's private train had drawn into a siding so that they could sleep without being disturbed, they lay close in a large bedstead which almost filled the sleeping-compartment, and Atayla said:

"I love you so much . . . and what you have made me feel is so wonderful . . . so perfect . . . so glorious that neither French nor Arabic, which are the only two languages I speak besides English, have . . . words to express it.

"Why should we need words?" the Earl asked in his deep voice. "But, my darling, tell me if I made you happy."

"So happy that I am still . . . flying in the . . . sky," Atayla answered passionately.

"I should be very frightened if that were true," the Earl said. "But I am holding you here safely in my arms, and I will never lose you, never let you go."

He drew a deep breath which was almost a sigh before he said:

"God certainly moves in a mysterious way! How could I have guessed that you would walk into my life so unexpectedly and change it so that I am not even sure if I am myself?"

"I want you just as you are," Atayla said. "No man could be more wonderful."

"You did not think that when you first met me."

"You frightened me," Atayla said. "At the same time, I thought no man could be so handsome, so distinguished . . . or so . . . masculine."

She paused before she added:

"When I came down to dinner when the Prince of Wales was there, I thought you were the one who looked Royal."

"You are flattering me!" the Earl exclaimed. "But I knew even then that you had turned my whole life upside-down, and although I was afraid to admit it, you were the Queen of my heart."

"Now you are flattering me!" Atayla whispered. "I have never presumed to be a Queen, but only to occupy the most important post in the world—that of your wife!"

The way she spoke made the Earl's lips seek hers, and for a moment as he touched them it was just a kiss of love and adoration.

Then as he felt her quiver against him and as her lips clung to his, their softness and innocence aroused an emotion in him different from anything he had ever known before.

He drew her closer still, and the fire within him leapt into flame.

To Atayla the love he had already given her was so perfect and so incredibly rapturous that she felt as if they were indivisibly one person and had no identity apart from each other.

While she knew their love was sacred, she was aware that at the same time he was teaching her about a love that invaded her like shafts of sunshine and vibrated through her until it was as if a light blazed from them both and grew and intensified with every breath they drew.

As he kissed her and his hands were touching her body, she could feel the strange sensations he had given her, which were unlike anything she had ever known existed, grow and intensify.

The fire on his lips was answered by the flames she felt within her, rising and rising until the Earl was lifting her into the sky and they were part of the blazing centre of the sun itself.

"You are mine!" she heard him say hoarsely, and his voice seemed very far away. "You are mine, my darling, from now until eternity, and I will never lose you."

"I am . . . yours!" Atayla replied. "Love me . . . please . . . love me . . . I am yours . . . all yours forever . . . and ever . . ."

Then the fires within them joined, and it was impossible to think.

The glory and wonder of it blinded their eyes, and there was only the radiance of the sun and the song of the angels.

ABOUT THE AUTHOR

Barbara Cartland, the world's most famous romantic novelist, who is also an historian, playwright, lecturer, political speaker and television personality, has now written over 350 books and sold over 350 million books throughout the world.

She has also had many historical works published and has written four autobiographies as well as the biographies of her mother and that of her brother, Ronald Cartland, who was the first Member of Parliament to be killed in World War II. This book has a preface by Sir Winston Churchill and has just been republished with an introduction by Sir Arthur Bryant.

Love at the Helm, a novel written with the help and inspiration of the late Earl Mountbatten of Burma, Uncle of His Royal Highness Prince Philip, is being sold for the Mountbatten Memorial Trust.

In 1978, Miss Cartland sang an Album of Love Songs with the Royal Philharmonic Orchestra.

In 1976, by writing twenty-one books, she broke the world record and has continued for the following five years with 24, 20, 23, 24, and 24. She is in the *Guinness Book of World Records* as the currently top-selling authoress in the world.

She is unique in that she was #1 and #2 in the Dalton List of Bestsellers, and one week had four books in the top twenty.

In private life Barbara Cartland, who is a Dame of the Order of St. John of Jerusalem, Chairman of the St. John Council in Hertfordshire and Deputy President of the St. John Ambulance Brigade, has also fought for better conditions and salaries for midwives and nurses.

Barbara Cartland is deeply interested in vitamin therapy and is President of the British National Association for Health. Her book, *The Magic of Honey*, has sold throughout the world and is translated into many languages.

Her designs, *Decorating with Love*, are being sold all over the USA and the National Home Fashions League made her "Woman of Achievement" in 1981.

Barbara Cartland Romances (book of cartoons) has just been published and seventy-five newspapers in the United States and several countries in Europe carry the strip cartoons of her novels.

Barbara Cartland

The world's bestselling author of romantic fiction. Her stories are always captivating tales of intrigue, adventure and love.